Young Dedalus
General Editor: Timothy La

THE GIRL FROM THE SEA AND OTHER STORIES

Sophia de Mello Breyner Andresen

The Girl from the Sea and other Stories

translated by Margaret Jull Costa
& Robin Patterson

Dedalus

Dedalus would like to thank the Direção-geral do Livro, dos Arquivos e das Bibliotecas, Portugal, and Arts Council England for their help in producing this translation.

DIREÇÃO-GERAL DO LIVRO, DOS ARQUIVOS E DAS BIBLIOTECAS

Published in the UK by Dedalus Limited
24-26, St Judith's Lane, Sawtry, Cambs, PE28 5XE
email: info@dedalusbooks.com
www.dedalusbooks.com

ISBN printed book 978 1 912868 03 2
ISBN ebook 978 1 912868 33 9

Dedalus is distributed in the USA & Canada by SCB Distributors
15608 South New Century Drive, Gardena, CA 90248
email: info@scbdistributors.com web: www.scbdistributors.com

Dedalus is distributed in Australia by Peribo Pty Ltd
58, Beaumont Road, Mount Kuring-gai, N.S.W. 2080
email: info@peribo.com.au

First published by Dedalus in 2020

Printed and bound in Great Britain by Clays Ltd, Elcograf S.p.A
Typeset by Marie Lane

A C.I.P. listing for this book is available on request.

The Author

Sophia de Mello Breyner Andresen - known simply as Sophia to Portuguese readers - was born in 1919 in the city of Porto in the north of Portugal. Her Danish grandfather, Jan Andresen had set sail from Denmark, disembarked in Porto and never left. He went on to become a very rich man and a leading figure in Porto society. Brought up in a wealthy Catholic family, Sophia always retained her religious faith, but was fiercely critical of Portugal's authoritarian Salazar regime, and became a member of parliament for the Socialist Party after the Carnation Revolution that overthrew the dictatorship in 1974. She published her first collection of poems in 1945 and went on to write many more, as well as short stories and translations, notably of Dante and Shakespeare. She became Portugal's most acclaimed poet of the twentieth century, and was the first woman to be awarded Portugal's highest literary honour, the Prémio Camões. She died in 2004.

Sophia had five children and originally wrote these stories for them. Like her poetry, the stories show a deep connection with the natural world, in particular with gardens and the sea. They are enjoyed by school children throughout Portugal to this day.

The Translators

Margaret Jull Costa has translated the works of many Spanish and Portuguese writers. She won the Portuguese Translation Prize for *The Book of Disquiet* by Fernando Pessoa in 1992 and for *The Word Tree* by Teolinda Gersão in 2012, and her translations of Eça de Queiroz's novels *The Relic* (1996) and *The City and the Mountains* (2009) were shortlisted for the prize; with Javier Marías, she won the 1997 International IMPAC Dublin Literary Award for *A Heart So White*, and, in 2000, she won the Oxford Weidenfeld Translation Prize for José Saramago's *All the Names*. In 2008 she won the Pen Book-of-the Month-Club Translation Prize and the Oxford Weidenfeld Translation Prize for *The Maias* by Eça de Queiroz.

Robin Patterson came late to literary translating, after pursuing other careers in various parts of the world. He has participated in both the Birkbeck and the BCLT literary translation summer schools and was mentored by Margaret Jull Costa in 2013 as part of the BCLT mentorship programme. His translated extracts from José Luís Peixoto's *Inside the Secret* were serialised in 2014 by Ninth Letter, and his translation of *Eve's Mango*, an extract from Vanessa da Mata's debut novel, was featured on the Bookanista website. He also contributed a translation of *Congressman Romário: Big Fish in the Aquarium* by Clara Becker to The Football Crónicas, a collection of football-related Latin American literature published by Ragpicker Press in June 2014. *Our Musseque* by José Luandino Vieira was his first translation for Dedalus.

Contents

THE GIRL FROM THE SEA

White house facing the vast sea,
With your garden of sand and sea flowers
And your unbroken silence in which sleeps
The miracle of the things that once were mine.

Once upon a time, there was a white house built in the dunes and facing the sea. It had a door, seven windows and a wooden balcony painted green. Surrounding the house was a sandy garden in which grew white lilies and another plant with white, yellow and red flowers.

In that house lived a boy who spent his days playing on the beach.

It was a very big beach, almost empty, apart from some marvellous rocks. At high tide, though, the rocks were under water, and all you could see were the waves growing and growing in the distance until they broke on the sand with a sound like people clapping. At low tide, the rocks became visible again, all covered in seaweed, whelks, anemones, limpets, algae and sea urchins. There were pools of water, streams, paths, grottoes, arches, waterfalls. There were pebbles of all shapes and colours, tiny and smooth and polished by the waves. The sea water was cold and transparent. Sometimes a fish swam by, almost too quick to be seen. You'd say to yourself: 'Look, a fish' and already it was gone. The jellyfish, though, drifted majestically past, opening and closing their red mantles. And the crabs scuttled all over the place, with furious faces and looking as if they were in a tremendous hurry.

The boy from the white house loved the rocks. He loved the green of the seaweed, the salt smell of the sea, the transparently cool waters. And that's why he felt really sad not to be a fish and able to swim down to the bottom of the sea without drowning. And he envied the seaweed bobbing on the currents, so light and so happy.

In September came the equinox, bringing with

it rough seas, gales, mists, rain and storms. The high tides swept up the beach as far as the dunes. One night, the waves roared and raged so loudly, and beat and broke so hard on the beach, that, in his whitewashed room in the white house, the boy lay awake into the small hours. The shutters on the windows rattled. The wooden floorboards creaked like ship's masts. It felt as if the waves were about to surround the house, and the sea was about to devour the whole world. And the boy imagined that, outside, in the dark night, a terrible battle was being waged, in which sea and sky and wind were brawling with each other. Finally, grown weary of listening, he fell asleep, lulled by the storm.

When he woke the next day, everything was calm again. The battle was over. The wind didn't moan, the sea didn't roar, there was only the gentle murmuring of small waves. The boy jumped out of bed, went over to the window and saw a lovely morning of bright sunshine, blue sky and blue sea. It was low tide. He put on his bathing trunks and ran down to the beach. Everything was so clear and quiet that he thought last night's storm must have been a dream.

But it wasn't. The beach was covered with foam from the stormy waves, row upon row of foam that trembled in the slightest breeze. It formed shapes like fantastical castles, white, but filled with a thousand other shimmering colours. When the boy touched them, the tremulous castles crumbled.

Then he went to play among the rocks. He began by following a thread of very clear water between two large dark rocks covered in whelks. The stream flowed into a large pool of water where the boy bathed and swam for a long time. Afterwards, he went scrabbling on over the rocks. He was heading for the south side of the beach, where there was never another soul to be seen. The tide was very low, and it was a beautiful morning. The seaweed seemed greener than ever, and the sea itself was tinged with lilac. The boy felt so happy that he sometimes broke into a dance. Now and then, he would find a really good pool and plunge in. When he'd already done this about ten times, he realised it must be time for him to go home. He climbed out of the pool and lay down on a rock in the sun.

'I really must go home,' he was thinking, but he didn't want to leave. And while he was lying there, his face resting on the seaweed, something extraordinary happened: he heard a very strange laugh, rather like the laugh you might hear from a bass baritone in an opera; then he heard a second

even stranger laugh, a tiny, brief laugh, more like a cough; this was followed by a third laugh, which sounded like someone in the water going 'glu glu glu'. The most extraordinary of all, though, was the fourth laugh, which was like a human laugh, only softer, finer, clearer. He'd never heard such a clear voice: it was as if water or glass were laughing.

Very carefully, so as not to make any noise, he stood up and peered out from his hiding place between two rocks. And there he saw a big octopus laughing, a crab laughing, a fish laughing and a tiny little girl laughing too. The little girl, who could only have been about a span high, had green hair, purple eyes and a dress made of scarlet seaweed. And the four of them were in a pool of very clean, clear water, surrounded by sea anemones. They were swimming and laughing.

'Ho, ho, ho,' laughed the octopus.

'Hee, hee, hee,' laughed the crab.

'Glu, glu, glu,' laughed the fish.

'Ha, ha, ha,' laughed the girl.

Then they stopped laughing, and the girl said: 'Now I want to dance.'

In an instant, the octopus, the crab and the fish transformed themselves into an orchestra.

The fish clapped his fins together in the water.

The crab climbed onto a rock and began to use his claws as castanets.

The octopus also clambered onto the rocks, where he stretched out seven of his eight arms, using his suckers to fasten the tip of each arm to the rock, and then, with his one free arm, he began to strum his other arms like the strings of a guitar. And then he began to sing.

The girl climbed out of the water onto another rock and started to dance. And the water coming and going around her feet danced too.

From his hiding place, the boy was watching, silent and motionless.

When the singing and dancing stopped, the octopus picked up the girl and began to rock her to sleep in his eight dark arms.

'The tide's coming in, it's time to leave,' said the crab.

'Yes, let's go,' said the octopus.

They summoned the fish, and the four of them set off. The fish swam ahead with the girl by his side, then came the octopus and, finally, the crab, still with that wary, angry look on his face.

They swam between the sand and the rocks until they reached a grotto and all four went in. The boy wanted to follow, but the entrance to the grotto

was very small, and he was far too big. And since the tide was coming in, he had to leave so as not to drown.

He went home feeling astonished at what he had seen, and all day he could think of nothing else. As soon as he woke the next morning, he ran down to the beach. He took the same path as before, and again hid behind the two rocks, and from there he watched and heard the same laughter as before. The girl, the crab, the octopus and the fish were dancing in a circle in the water. They were having such fun.

Mad with curiosity, the boy couldn't bear to sit there doing nothing any more. He lunged forward and grabbed the girl.

'No, no!' she cried.

Terrified, the octopus, the crab and the fish all vanished in the twinkling of an eye.

'Octopus, crab, fish, help me, please! Save me!' cried the girl.

Then, overcoming their fear, the octopus, crab and fish emerged from behind the seaweed where they had hidden and began to try and save the girl. They did their best: the octopus climbed up the boy's legs, the crab pinched his feet with his claws, and the fish nipped at his shins. However, since the boy was bigger and stronger than them, he simply dealt them a few kicks and ran away with the girl, who continued to call out: 'Octopus! Crab! Fish!'

'Don't scream and don't cry and don't be frightened,' said the boy. 'I'm not going to hurt you.'

'Yes, you are.'

'How could I possibly hurt a pretty little girl like you?'

'You're going to cook me and eat me,' said the girl from the sea, and again began crying and screaming. 'Octopus! Crab! Fish!'

'Cook you and eat you! Why would I do that? What a strange idea!' said the boy, horrified.

'The fish say that men cook and eat everything they catch.'

The boy burst out laughing and said: 'Oh, the fishermen do. They're the ones who catch the fish and cook them. But I'm not a fisherman and you're not a fish. I don't want to cook you or hurt you in any way. I just want to have a proper look at you, because I've never seen such a tiny pretty little girl before. I want you to tell me who you are, how you live, and what you're doing here in the sea and what your name is.'

Then the girl stopped screaming, wiped away her tears, combed and smoothed her hair with her fingers and said: 'Let's go and sit down on that rock, and I'll tell you everything.'

'Promise you won't run away?'

'I promise.'

They sat facing each other, and the girl began: 'I'm a girl from the sea. My name is Girl from the Sea and I have no other name. I don't know where I was born. One day, a seagull carried me in its beak and brought me to this beach. He set me down on a rock at low tide, and the octopus, the crab and the fish took care of me. The four of us live in a very pretty cave. The octopus does the housework, smoothes the sand and fetches the food. He's the one who works hardest, because he has so many arms. The crab is the chef. He makes seaweed broth, foam icecream, kelp salad, turtle soup, caviar and lots of other things. He's a really excellent chef. When the food is ready, the octopus lays the table. The table cloth is a piece of white seaweed, and the plates are shells. Then, at night, the octopus makes up my bed with some more seaweed, very green and very soft. But the crab is my seamstress. And he's also my jeweller: he makes me necklaces out of shells and coral and pearls. The fish doesn't do anything, because he doesn't have hands like me, or arms with suckers like the octopus, or claws like the crab. He only has fins, and fins are only good for swimming.

But he's my best friend. Since he doesn't have arms, he never punishes me. He's my playmate. When it's low tide, we play among the rocks, and when it's high tide, we go for walks on the bottom of the sea. You won't ever have been to the bottom of the sea, so you can't possibly know how lovely it is there. There are forests of kelp, gardens of anemones, fields of shells. There are seahorses suspended like question marks in the water, with a look of astonishment on their faces. There are flowers that resemble animals and animals that resemble flowers. There are mysterious grottoes, dark blues, purples, greens and endless expanses of fine, white, smooth sand. You're from the land, and if you went to the bottom of the sea, you would drown. But I'm a girl from the sea. I can breathe under water like a fish and breathe out of the water too, like people. And I have the whole ocean at my disposal and can do what I like, and no one will hurt me because I dance for the Great Ray. And the Great Ray is the mistress of these waters. She's huge, big enough to swallow a boat with ten men on board. She looks really nasty and eats men and fish and is always hungry. She doesn't eat me because she says I'm too small and no good for eating, but that I'm very good at dancing. And the Ray loves to see me dance. Whenever she gives a party, she invites the sharks and the whales, and they all sit on the bottom of the sea and I dance for them into the small hours. And when the Ray is sad or feeling indisposed, then I have to dance in order to cheer her up. That's why I'm a sea-dancer and can do what I want and it's why everyone likes me. But I don't like the Ray at all, and I'm afraid of her. She hates men and doesn't like fish either. Even the whales are afraid of her. But I can wander the sea as I wish and no one eats me and no one hurts me because I am the Great Ray's dancer. And now that I've told you my story, take me back to my friends, who must be terribly worried.'

The boy very carefully placed the girl on the palm of his hand and took her back to where she had come from. The octopus, the crab and the fish were all huddled together, weeping.

'I'm back,' shouted the Girl from the Sea.

As soon as they saw her, the octopus, the crab and the fish stopped crying and hurled themselves, like three dogs, at the boy's feet, with the crab and the fish nipping and pinching him, while the octopus with his eight arms lashed at the boy's legs.

'Stop it, don't hurt him, he's my friend and he's not going to cook me and eat me,' said the Girl from the Sea. Utterly amazed at these words, the octopus, the crab and the fish stopped their assault on the boy. The boy bent down and placed the girl in the water next to her three friends, who were now leaping up and down with joy and laughing loudly. The tide was coming in, and the boy had to leave. He asked the girl, the octopus, the crab and the fish to come back the next day, at the same hour, in that same place.

'I'm so curious to see the land,' said the girl. 'When you come tomorrow, bring me something from the land.'

And so it was.

The following day, early in the morning, the boy went into his garden to pick a highly scented red rose. He went down to the beach and looked for the place where he had met them the previous day.

'Good morning, good morning, good morning, good morning,' said the girl, the octopus, the crab and the fish.

'Good morning,' said the boy. And he knelt down in the water, opposite the Girl from the Sea.

'I've brought you a flower from the land,' he said, 'it's called a rose.'

'Oh, it's lovely,' said the Girl from the Sea, gleefully clapping her hands and dancing round the rose.

'Smell it and you'll see how perfumed it is.'

She put her head inside the rose petals and took a long breath.

Then she looked up and said with a sigh: 'What a marvellous perfume. There's nothing like that in the sea. But it makes me feel dizzy and a little sad. The things of the land are strange. They're different from the things of the sea. In the sea there are all kinds of monsters and dangers, but the pretty things are pure joy. On the land, there's sadness even in the prettiest things.'

'In Portuguese, that's what we call *saudade,*' said the boy.

'What's *saudade*?' asked the girl.

'*Saudade* is the sadness that lingers inside us when we lose the things we love.'

'Oh!' sighed the Girl from the Sea, looking back at the land. 'Why did you show me that rose? I feel like crying now.'

The boy threw the rose away and said: 'Forget about the rose and let's go and play.'

And off the five of them went, the boy, the girl, the octopus, the crab and the fish, along the watery paths, where they spent the whole morning laughing and having fun.

Until the tide began to come in, and the boy had

to leave.

The following morning, they met again in what was now the usual place.

'Good morning,' said the girl. 'What have you brought me today?'

The boy picked her up, sat her on a rock and knelt beside her.

'I brought you this,' he said. 'It's a box of matches.'

'It's not very pretty,' said the girl.

'No, but it contains something marvellous, beautiful and joyful called fire. Let me show you.'

And the boy opened the box and lit a match.

The girl clapped her hands in delight and asked if she could touch the fire.

'No,' said the boy, 'that's impossible. The fire is a joyful thing, but it burns.'

'It's like a little sun,' said the Girl from the Sea.

'Yes,' said the boy, 'but you can't touch it.'

And he blew on the match and the fire went out.

'You're a wizard,' said the girl. 'You blow on things and they vanish.'

'I'm not a wizard. That's just what fire is like. When it's small, anyone can blow it out. But when it gets big, it can devour whole forests and cities.'

'So is fire even worse than the Great Ray?' asked

the girl.

'That depends. As long as the fire is small and sensible, then it's man's best friend: it warms him in winter, cooks his food for him, gives him light at night. But when the fire grows too big, it becomes angry and unhinged, and then it's crueller and more dangerous than even the fiercest of beasts.'

'The things of the land are strange and different,' said the Girl from the Sea. 'Tell me about some more things.'

Then they sat down in the water, and the boy told her what his house and garden were like and about cities and fields, forests and roads.

'Oh, how I wish I could see all those things,' said the girl, brimming with curiosity.

'Come with me,' said the boy. 'I'll take you to the land and show you all kinds of lovely things.'

'I can't, because I'm a girl from the sea. The sea is my land. If you came to visit me in the sea you would drown. And so would I if I went on dry land. I can't spend much time out of the water. Out of the water, I become like the seaweed at low tide, all dry and wrinkled. If I were to leave the sea, after only a few hours, I would be just like an old rag or a scrap of newspaper, the kind of thing you find on the beach sometimes and which always looks so sad and lonely, like something that's no use any more and has been thrown away, unwanted by anyone.'

'It's such a shame that I can't show you the land!' said the boy.

'And such a shame that I can't take you with me to the bottom of the sea and show you the seaweed forests and the coral caves and the gardens of anemones!'

And that morning, as they swam in the water, the boy and the girl told each other stories of the sea and stories of the land.

Until the tide came in and they had to say goodbye.

The following day, the boy came to the beach, sat down beside the Girl from the Sea and said: 'Today I've brought you something from the land that is both pretty and joyful. It's called wine. Anyone who drinks it is filled with joy.'

While he was speaking, the boy placed on the sand a glass full of wine. It was one of those very small glasses used for liqueurs. The Girl from the Sea picked up the glass with both hands and studied the wine very curiously, breathing in its perfume...

'It's very red and very perfumed,' she said. 'Tell me what wine is.'

'On the land,' answered the boy, 'there's a

plant called a vine. In the winter, it looks dead and withered, but in the spring, it sprouts lots of leaves and in the summer it's full of fruit called grapes, which grow in bunches. And in the autumn, men pick the bunches of grapes and put them in big stone tanks where they tread on them to extract the juice. And it's the juice from that fruit that we call wine. That is the story of wine, but I don't know how to describe its taste. Take a sip if you want to know.'

And the girl took a sip of wine, giggled and said: 'It's really very nice and very jolly. Now I know what the land is like. Now I know the taste of spring, summer and autumn. Now I know what the fruit tastes like. Now I know the coolness of the trees. Now I know the heat of a mountain in the sun. Take me to see the land. I want to see it. There are so many things I don't know. The sea is a transparent, frozen prison. There's no spring or autumn in the sea. In the sea, time doesn't die. The anemones are always in flower and the foam is always white. Take me to see the land.'

'I have an idea,' said the boy. 'Tomorrow I'll bring a bucket and fill it with sea water and seaweed. And you can sit in the bucket so that you don't dry up, and I'll take you to see the land.'

'All right,' said the girl. 'Tomorrow, I'll come with you in the bucket of water. And I'll go and see your house and your garden and watch the trains passing and see night in a city full of lights and people and cars. And I'll go and see the animals of the land, dogs, horses, cats; and I'll see the mountains, the forests and all the other things you've told me about.'

And so the boy and the Girl from the Sea spent the rest of the morning planning the next day's adventure. Until the tide came in, and the boy had to leave.

The next day, the boy came to the rocks carrying a bucket. He was in high spirits, singing and skipping, excited about his plan for the day, but when he reached the usual pool of water, he found the Girl from the Sea in deep despair, and the octopus, the crab and the fish looking very worried.

'Good morning,' said the boy. 'I've brought the bucket. Let's go.'

'I can't,' said the Girl from the Sea. And she burst into floods of tears.

'But why not?' asked the boy.

'Because of the whelks. They have very good hearing, and they hear everything, they're the ears of the sea. And they overheard our conversation and went and told the Great Ray, who was furious, and now I can't go with you.'

'But the Great Ray isn't here. Get in the bucket and let's go.'

'That's just not possible,' said the Girl from the Sea. 'The Great Ray ordered the octopuses not to let me pass. The rocks are full of hidden octopuses that we can't see, but who are watching our every move. I must say goodbye to you for ever. I won't be here tomorrow, because, to punish me for wanting to run away, the Ray has decided that tonight at moonrise, I will be taken by the octopuses to a remote beach, whose name and location I don't even know. And we will never be able to meet again.'

'Let's try and escape,' said the boy. 'I can run faster on my two legs than the octopuses can on their eight arms, which are neither arms nor legs.'

And with that, he put the Girl from the Sea in the bucket and set off at a run. At that same moment, though, the rocks were suddenly swarming with octopuses. Wherever he looked there were octopuses. He searched for some opening where he could get through, but there was none. The octopuses had formed a tight circle around them. And he was in the middle of that circle and could not escape. Then he tried to jump over the octopuses, but immediately dozens of tentacles twined about his legs.

'Let me go, let me go,' said the Girl from the Sea. 'Let me go or they'll kill you.'

'No, I won't let you go,' said the boy.

But the octopuses had wrapped their arms about his waist and chest, grasped his shoulders, bound his wrists, and he fell, helpless, onto the rocks. He still had hold of the bucket though, until, that is, an octopus put one tentacle around his throat and began to squeeze. The boy saw the sky turn black, he could no longer hear the sound of the waves, and, finally, he forgot everything. He lost consciousness. He woke to feel the water lapping on his face. The tide had come in, and the waves had almost covered the rocks where he had fallen. He stood up, and his whole body still ached and was covered with the marks left by the octopuses' suckers. He slowly made his way home.

Days and more days passed. The boy often returned to the rocks, but he never again saw the girl or her three friends there. It was as if it had all been a dream.

Then winter arrived. The weather was cold, the sea grey and it rained nearly every day. One misty morning, the boy sat down on the beach to think about the Girl from the Sea.

And while he was doing this, he saw a seagull flying in from the sea carrying something in his beak. That something was shiny, and glinted in the light. The boy thought it must be a fish. But the seagull came very close, circled him in the air, then dropped the object on the sand.

The boy picked it up and saw that it was a bottle full of a very clear, luminous liquid.

'Good morning,' said the seagull.

'Good morning,' said the boy. 'Where have you come from and why are you giving me this bottle?'

'I'm here at the request of the Girl from the Sea,' said the seagull. 'She told me to tell you that now she understands the meaning of *saudade*. And she asked me to ask you if you'd like to meet her at the bottom of the sea.'

'Oh, I would, I would,' said the boy. 'But how can I go to the bottom of the sea without drowning?'

'The bottle I gave you contains the juice of sea anemones and of other magical plants too. If you drink this potion, you will become like the Girl from the Sea. You will be able to live in the water like a fish and out of the water like people.'

'I'll drink it now,' said the boy.

And he drank the potion.

Everything around him seemed to become brighter and more brilliant. He felt as happy, joyful and contented as a fish. It was as if something about the way he moved had become freer, stronger, fresher and lighter.

'Out there in the sea,' said the seagull, 'is a dolphin waiting to show you the way.'

The boy looked and saw a large glossy black dolphin leaping about among the waves. Then he said.

'Goodbye, seagull. And thank you so much.'

And he ran into the waves and swam out to the dolphin.

'Hold onto my tail,' said the dolphin.

And the two headed out to sea.

They swam for many days and many nights through calms and storms.

They crossed the wide Sargasso Sea and saw flying fish. They saw huge whales sending spouts of water up into the sky and saw great steamships that left columns of smoke hanging in the air behind them. And they saw majestic white icebergs in the lonely ocean wastes. And they swam beside swift sailing ships, sails taut in the wind. And the sailors cried out in amazement when they saw a boy hanging on to the tail of a dolphin. But the boy and dolphin dived deep down so as not to be caught. There they saw old shipwrecks with their coffers full of gold and their broken masts encrusted with sea anemones and shells.

After swimming for sixty days and sixty nights, they reached an island surrounded by coral. The dolphin swam around the island and finally stopped outside a grotto and said: 'Here we are, if you go inside, you'll find the Girl from the Sea.'

'Goodbye, dolphin. And thank you so much.'

The cave was made all of coral, and the floor of fine, white sand. Outside was a garden of blue anemones. The boy went into the cave and peered about him. The girl, the octopus, the crab and the fish were playing with little shells. They were very still and sad and silent. Now and then, the girl would sigh.

'I'm here! I've arrived! It's me!' cried the boy.

They all turned to look at him. For a moment there was great confusion. Then they all embraced and laughed and shouted. The Girl from the Sea danced, clapping and laughing, and her laughter was as clear as water. The octopus did a handstand, the crab performed somersaults, and the fish did back flips. Finally, after all these high jinks, they calmed down a little.

Then the Girl from the Sea sat on the boy's shoulder and said: 'I am so, so, so happy! I thought I would never see you again. Without you, the sea, despite all its anemones, seemed sad and empty. And I would spend whole days just sighing. I didn't know what to do. Until one day, the King of the Sea gave a big party. He invited a lot of whales and sharks and a lot of important fish. And he ordered me to go to the palace to dance at the party. At the end of the banquet, it was my turn to dance, and I went into the grotto where the King of the Sea was seated on his mother-of-pearl throne, surrounded by his guests and by seahorses. Then the whelks began singing a very ancient song, composed at the very beginning of the world. But I was really sad and so I danced really badly.

"Why are you dancing so badly?" asked the King of the Sea.

"Because I'm full of *saudade*," I replied.

"*Saudade*?" said the King of the Sea. "Whatever's that?"

And he asked the octopus, the crab and the fish what had happened. They told him everything. Then the King of the Sea felt sorry for me in my sadness and felt sad to see a dancer who could no longer dance. And he said: "Come to my palace tomorrow morning."

The following morning, I went back to the palace. And the King of the Sea sat me on his shoulder and swam up to the surface with me. He summoned a seagull, gave him the bottle with the anemone juice potion and sent him off to find you. And that is how I got you to come back.'

'Now we'll never be parted again,' said the boy.

'Now you'll be as strong as an octopus,' said the octopus.

'Now you'll be as wise as a crab,' said the crab.

'Now you'll be as happy as a fish,' said the fish.

'Now your land is the sea,' said the Girl from the Sea.

And the five of them set off through forests and grottoes and sand.

The following day, there was another party at the King's palace. The Girl from the Sea danced all night, and the whales, the sharks, the turtles and all the fishes said: 'We never saw anyone dance so well.'

And the King of the Sea was seated on his mother-of-pearl throne, surrounded by seahorses, and his purple mantle floated in the water.

The Fairy Oriana

Good Fairies and Bad Fairies

There are two kinds of fairy: good fairies and bad fairies. The good fairies do good things and the bad fairies do bad things.

The good fairies water the flowers with dew, light the fire for old people, catch children about to fall into the river, bewitch gardens, dance in the air, invent dreams and, at night, place gold coins in the shoes of the poor.

The bad fairies make fountains dry up, douse the fires lit by shepherds, deliberately tear to shreds washing hung out in the sun to dry, unbewitch gardens, tease children, torment animals and steal money from the poor.

When a good fairy sees a dead tree, with its branches all bare and withered, she touches it with her magic wand and the tree is instantly covered with leaves, flowers, fruit and singing birds.

When a bad fairy sees a tree full of leaves, flowers, fruit and singing birds, she touches it with her magic wand, and an icy wind instantly whips off the leaves, the fruits rot, the flowers wither and the birds fall to the ground dead.

Oriana

Once upon a time there was a fairy called Oriana, She was a good fairy and very pretty. She lived free and happy and contented, dancing in the fields, over the hills, in the woods, the gardens and on the beaches.

One day, the Fairy Queen called to her and said: 'Oriana, come with me.'

And together they flew over plains, lakes and mountains, until they reached a country where there was a great forest.

'Oriana,' said the Fairy Queen, 'I give you this forest. From now on, all the people, animals and plants that live here are under your protection. You are the fairy of this forest. Promise me that you will never abandon it.'

Oriana said: 'I promise.'

And from then on, Oriana lived in that forest. At night, she would sleep in a hollow in the trunk of an oak tree. In the morning, she would wake up very early, even earlier than the flowers and the birds. Her alarm clock was the first ray of sun. For she had a lot to do. Everyone in the forest needed her. She warned the rabbits and the deer when the hunters were about to arrive. She watered the flowers with dew. She took care of the miller's eleven children. She freed the birds that got caught in the mousetraps.

At night, when everyone was sleeping, Oriana would go to the fields and dance with the other fairies. Or she would fly alone above the forest, and, spreading her wings, would hover in the air between earth and sky. All around the forest lay silently sleeping fields and mountains. In the distance, she could see the lights of a city hunched beside its river. By day, and seen from close to, the city was dark, ugly and sad, but, by night, it glittered with lights - green, purple, yellow, blue, red and lilac - as if there were a party going on. The city, then, seemed to be made of opals, rubies, diamonds, emeralds and sapphires.

A summer passed, an autumn passed, a winter passed, then spring arrived. And one April morning, Oriana woke even earlier than usual. As soon as the first ray of sun penetrated the forest, she emerged from inside the trunk of the oak tree where she slept. She breathed in the perfumes of dawn and performed a little jig. Then she combed her hair with her fingers and washed her face with dew.

'What a beautiful morning!' she said. 'I've never known a morning as blue, as green, as fresh and golden as this.'

She danced through the forest, saying good morning to everything. First, the trees woke, then the cockerels, then the birds, then the flowers, then the rabbits, then the deer and the foxes, and, finally, the people. And that was when Oriana went to visit the old lady.

She was a very old old lady who lived in a very old old house. And there was nothing inside the house but rags, rickety furniture and cracked china. Oriana peered through the window, which had no glass. The old lady was tidying the house and, while she worked, she talked to herself, saying: 'What a dreadful life, what a wretched life! I'm as old as time itself and yet I still have to work. And I have no son or daughter to help me. If it wasn't for the fairies, what would become of me?

'When I was little, I used to play in the forest, and the animals, the leaves and the flowers would play with me. My mother would comb my hair and pin a ribbon on my dress to dance along with me. Now, if it wasn't for the fairies, what would become of me?

'When I was young, I would spend the whole day laughing. At dances, I would dance all night. I had friends by the dozen. Now I'm old and have no one. If it wasn't for the fairies, what would become of me?

'When I was young, I had suitors who would tell me how pretty I was and throw carnations at me when I passed. Now little boys chase after me, calling me "old hag" and throw stones at me. If it wasn't for the fairies, what would become of me?

'When I was young, I had a palace, silk dresses, valets and footmen. Now I'm old and have nothing. If it wasn't for the fairies, what would become of me?'

Oriana heard this same lament every morning, and every morning, she felt sad and full of pity for this old lady, so bent and wrinkled and alone, who spent all day complaining and sighing.

Fairies only show themselves to children, animals, trees and flowers. That's why the old lady never actually saw Oriana, but even though she couldn't see her, she knew she was there, ready to help.

Once the old lady had swept the house, she lit the fire and put water on to boil. Then she opened the tin of coffee and said: 'I have no coffee.'

Oriana touched the tin with her magic wand, and the tin filled up with coffee.

The old lady made herself some coffee, then picked up the milk jug and said: 'I have no milk.'

Oriana touched the jug with her magic wand, and the jug filled up with milk.

The old lady picked up the sugar bowl and said: 'I have no sugar.'

Oriana touched the bowl with her magic wand, and the bowl filled up with sugar.

The old lady opened the bread bin and said: 'I have no bread.'

Oriana touched the bin with her magic wand and a loaf and butter appeared.

The old lady picked up the loaf and said: 'If it wasn't for the fairies what would become of me?'

And when Oriana heard this, she smiled.

The old lady ate and drank and then, with a sigh, said: 'Now I must go to work.'

'Work' meant picking up kindling that she would later sell in the city.

And every morning Oriana would help her collect the fallen twigs and branches and every morning she would guide her into the city, because the old lady's eyesight was very poor, and the path from the forest to the city was flanked by deep ravines, into which the old lady could easily have fallen had Oriana not been there to guide her.

And so, on that April morning, Oriana and the old lady walked together down the path, with the old lady very bent and leaning on a stick, and Oriana flying through the air like a butterfly. And without the old lady noticing, Oriana lifted up the bundle of kindling so that it weighed less heavily on the old lady's bent back.

When they reached the city, the old lady went from door to door selling the firewood, and Oriana flew up onto a roof, where she sat gazing down at the houses, waiting for her friend. While she was waiting, she talked to the swallows: 'Those far-off lands are wonderful,' they told her.

'Tell me about them,' said Oriana.

'The King of Siam has a palace with a golden roof, and in China there are towers made of porcelain,' said one swallow.

'In Oceania there are coral islands thick with grass and palm trees. And on those islands, people wear flowers and are pretty, kind and happy,' said another.

'Kangaroos have a pocket in which they keep their children, and the King of Tibet can read other men's minds,' said yet another swallow.

'High up in the Andes there are abandoned cities, inhabited only by eagles and snakes,' said another swallow.

'How marvellous! Tell me everything,' Oriana begged them.

'We can't tell you everything,' said the swallows. 'There are so many marvellous things in the world. Why don't you come with us, Oriana? We leave when autumn arrives. You have wings too. Come with us.'

But Oriana looked up at the vast transparent dome of the sky and sighed: 'No, I can't. The people and animals and plants of the forest need me.'

'But you have wings, Oriana. You can fly over oceans and mountains. You can fly to the other side of the world. There's so much space out there. It would be so good if you could come. You could fly very high, above the clouds, or you could fly over the surface of the blue sea, dipping the tips of your toes into the cold water of the waves. And you could fly over virgin forests, breathing in the perfume of unknown flowers and fruits. You would see cities, mountains, rivers, deserts and oases. In the middle of the great Ocean, there are tiny islands with beaches of fine white sand. There, on moonlit nights, everything is blue and still and silvery. Imagine that, Oriana!'

But Oriana, looking up at the high sky and the drifting clouds, sighed and said: 'Imagine what would become of the old lady if she woke up one cold morning and found no bread and no milk.'

'Come with us, Oriana,' the swallows said again.

'I promised I would take care of the forest,' she answered, 'and a promise is a very important thing.'

Then the swallows looked at her with hard, dark, brilliant eyes and said very sternly: 'Oriana, you don't deserve to have wings. You don't love the open spaces, you scorn freedom.'

Oriana bowed her head and answered: 'I made a promise.'

The swallows turned their backs on her and did not speak to her again.

Once the old lady had sold her kindling, she left the city, accompanied by Oriana, and they both walked back to the forest.

It was almost midday by the time they got there, and Oriana then left her and went to the woodman's house.

The woodman was very poor. In his house he

had only a bed, a fireplace, a table and three benches.

The door was always open because there was nothing worth stealing.

Before going in, Oriana picked up three small white stones.

The house was very clean and tidy because the woodman's wife liked everything to be just right. Besides, there was very little to tidy.

Oriana flew around the house to see what was needed.

She opened the bread bin and saw that there was still bread, and so she closed it again.

Then she opened the clothes drawer. There were not many clothes and they were hardly new, but they were all clean and darned. There was one blouse, though, that was so old and had so many holes in it that even darning wouldn't help. Oriana put one small white stone in the drawer, touched it with her magic wand, and the stone became a brand-new blouse.

Then Oriana opened the money box and saw that it was empty. She put a small white stone inside and it became a nice round new coin.

And underneath the table lay the ball that the woodman's son played with. Oriana picked it up and, seeing how worn and battered it was, she put the third white stone under the table and changed it into a new ball.

Oriana went to the woodman's house almost every day. She always took three small white stones with her and changed them into anything that was needed. And the woodman's wife would say to her husband: 'Who is the kind person who comes to our house when I'm out and brings me the things I need?'

Oriana left the woodman's house and thought: 'Today is market day. The miller will have gone into the city to sell his flour. His wife will have gone with him and taken their eleven children too. I'll go to their house and see if there's anything they need.'

And she went to the miller's house.

The door was locked, but Oriana touched the lock with her magic wand and the door opened.

The house was in a terrible state. Everything was higgledy-piggledy and covered in flour. Nothing was in its right place, because the miller's wife had eleven children and was untidy and absent-minded, and never had time to do anything. If it hadn't been for Oriana, the house would have been uninhabitable.

Oriana went in and looked around. She sighed to see such disorder. Then she went to fetch a broom and a duster and swept and cleaned the whole house. With her magic wand she glued together all the broken things. She washed the dishes and put them away in the cupboards. She brushed all the coats and hung them up. She mended all the clothes in the laundry basket and repaired the broken toys.

When she had finished, she looked around. The house was lovely, tidy and clean. Oriana smiled and left.

Oriana tidied the miller's house almost every day, but the miller's wife never noticed, because she was always late leaving the house and always in a hurry. And because she was so distracted, she didn't even notice that it was untidy and higgledy-piggledly. And when she returned home, she wasn't surprised to find everything tidy again, because she wasn't even aware that the house had been a mess when she left.

Oriana left the miller's house and went to the Very Rich Man's house.

The Very Rich Man

The Very Rich Man had no wife, no children and no friends. All he had were servants.

His house was in the middle of an immaculately kept garden, with a lawn, shrubs, flowers and sandy paths.

Oriana walked round the house to find a way in. All the doors were locked, and Oriana couldn't open them, because the locks in the Very Rich Man's house were so expensive that not even a magic wand could open them. There was, however, one window open. It was the living-room window. Oriana peered in and saw that there was no one there, only an awful lot of furniture and a very tense atmosphere. The sofas and the chairs kept elbowing each other, the sideboards kicked against the walls, the vases told the various caskets and ashtrays not to crowd them, while the flowers said: 'I can't stand it any more, I can't breathe!'

The room was as full to the brim as an egg.

Oriana went in, and the furnishings all started talking at once.

'Oriana, Oriana, get us out of here,' yelled the flowers.

'Oriana, tell that vase to stop crowding me,' said the casket.

'Oriana, tell the table not to tread on me so hard,' said the rug.

'Oriana, tell the sofa to stop elbowing me,' said the chair.

'Oriana, tell the screen to move further off,' said the wall.

'Oriana,' said the mirror, 'get me out of here. This room is so crowded and cramped that my glass eyes are sore and weary with seeing everything all the time.'

'Calm down, and don't all talk at once,' said Oriana.

They fell silent, then the table said: 'Oriana, we can't stay here. There isn't enough space. There are too many things in here. We're too squashed together. And we're all very different and don't necessarily get on. I, for example, am a very old table and started life in a convent refectory. True, I am very long, but the refectory was so spacious that I fitted in perfectly, because, apart from me, there were only benches. I don't like it here. The other bits of furniture are always bumping into me. That gilt sofa and I have fallen out already, because while I'm all smooth, he's all curves and curlicues. We simply have nothing in common. I'm a convent table, I took a vow of poverty, and I can't live in this room. Oriana, touch me with your magic wand and take me back to where I belong.'

Then the sideboard spoke.

'I'm a very pretty, very old sideboard. For two centuries I lived in a very large room in a very large country house, and anyone who entered could see at once how lovely I was. During the day, I would hear children laughing in the garden or chasing each other down the corridor. At night, all I heard was the singing of the wind and the frogs and the splashing of the fountain. When they held parties, the house would be full of lights. People would walk past me and say: "What a lovely sideboard!"

And the owner of the house would answer: "Yes, my father had it made specially."

A few decades later, the owner would say: "Yes, my grandfather had it made specially."

More decades passed and the owner would say: "Yes, my great-grandfather had it made specially."

Still more decades passed and the owner would say: "Yes, my great-great-grandfather had it made specially."

You see, I was passed on from generation to generation. And I knew the parents, the children, the grandchildren and the grandchildren's grandchildren. I was a member of the family. Everyone wept when I was sold. The trees' tears fell drop by drop onto the ground, and their leaves waved a thousand farewells. Here, it's different. Here, no one is my friend, neither the people nor the objects. When anyone says to the owner how very lovely I am, he replies: "Yes, I got it for a knock-down price." Oriana, take me away from here. Take me back to that room in the country house.'

Then the mirror spoke: 'I used to live in a palace where there was nothing but empty space all around me. And the floor was made of smooth, shining marble. I stood at the far end of a silent, solitary gallery. And I would watch as the hours of the day slipped by. I saw kings and queens, pale-faced on their coronation day, wearing their heavy, glittering crowns. I saw ministers, counsellors, and important men with their long noses, solemn faces and obsequious manners. And I saw young women in their white dresses who, on nights when balls were held, would escape for an instant into the empty gallery. They would skip along so quickly and lightly, always refusing to surrender the flower their suitors asked them for. And I saw the desperate revolutionary hordes pass through in their search for justice, smashing everything in sight. I saw and saw and saw.

'I am a mirror. I have spent my whole life seeing. All those images entered into me. I saw and saw and saw. And now I'm stuck in this room where there's nowhere for my eyes to rest. Oriana, take me away from here and put me in front of a smooth, bare, white wall.'

And one by one, all the other objects begged her to take them somewhere else.

'My dears,' said Oriana, 'I simply cannot do what you ask. If I were to take you away from here, the owner of the house would be most upset. And I can't go into a house and upset the owner.'

'So what are we going to do?' they all asked.

'Nothing,' said Oriana. 'Everything in this room has such a hopeless air about it. When I go into other houses, I can provide whatever is lacking, but here nothing is lacking. There's too much of everything. I would actually have to remove things, but I can't go into a house and remove what's there.'

'Well, if you can't take us away, then make the room bigger so that we can all fit in.'

'I'm terribly sorry,' said Oriana, 'but that's impossible too. When the owner of this house had it built, he said to the architect: "Make me a small, modest house, so that other people won't feel envious."'

The furnishings fell silent for a moment, thinking, then they said: 'Oriana, why not persuade the owner to give us away as a present to someone who has no furniture.'

'Now that,' said Oriana, 'is an excellent idea. I know exactly what I can do.'

There was a notepad and pen on the table. Oriana picked up the pen and wrote:

He who gives to the poor gives to God. Give half of your furniture to the poor.

'Excellent,' said the furniture.

'Oriana,' said the mirror, 'could you just remove that Saxe figurine of a dancer. I'm sick to death of seeing her there, with one foot in the air as if she might topple over at any moment. Since I have no eyelids, the nights are my only eyelids. During the day, though, I can't close my eyes. And I'm tired of spending all day every day staring at a dancer with one foot in the air.'

The dancer was on a shelf opposite the mirror. Oriana picked her up and placed her on the other side of the room, on top of the sideboard, where the mirror couldn't see her.

'Thank you,' said the mirror.

Footsteps were heard in the corridor, and Oriana hid behind the screen.

The door opened and in came the Very Rich Man.

The first thing he saw was the notepad on the table, and when he read what was written, he was furious, because he was very very mean. He exclaimed: 'What a nerve!'

Then, when he saw that the dancer had been moved, he was outraged and rang the bell to summon his butler.

'Tell the servants to come here at once,' said the Very Rich Man.

A moment later, the servants arrived. They stood in a line at the door. Turning his back on the notepad on the table and on the sideboard where the dancer was now poised, the Very Rich Man declared: 'Two truly shocking things have happened in this house, and woe betide whoever was responsible! I want the guilty party to confess. I want to know who wrote that message on the notepad and who moved the dancer.'

The servants were all terrified, and Oriana was aghast at the consequences of her actions. In the twinkling of an eye, she touched the notepad with her magic wand, making the words vanish, then touched the dancer, making her fly back to the shelf.

The Very Rich Man picked up the notepad, again turned to the servants and said: 'Who wrote this?'

The servants stared at the blank sheet of paper and said: 'There's nothing there.'

The Very Rich Man thought he must be dreaming.

He didn't know what to say or how to react. He cleared his throat, then asked in a very stern voice: 'Who removed the dancer from that shelf?'

But when he looked at the shelf, the dancer was in her usual place. I must be going mad, he thought. Angry and embarrassed to be making such a fool of himself in front of the servants, he again cleared his throat and said: 'I was just testing. You can go now.'

The servants left, and the Very Rich Man sat down on a chair and began talking to himself: 'There must have been some kind of sleight of hand, so skilfully done that I didn't notice a thing. It must have been the maid. Right now, they'll all be in the kitchen laughing at me. I must dismiss that maid at once.'

Oriana was horrified.

'What a dreadful place,' she was thinking. 'Here, everything turns out badly. I can't seem to help anyone.'

While she was thinking this, she peered over the top of the screen. The Very Rich Man was sitting with his back to her, and Oriana saw that he was as bald as an egg. Then she felt sorry for him and decided to give him the gift of some hair. With her magic wand she touched his bald head, which immediately became covered in thousands of very fine, very short hairs. The Very Rich Man felt his head itching. He went over to the mirror to see what it was, and saw that he had a full head of newly sprouted hair.

At first, he couldn't believe his eyes. He stood for a moment, open-mouthed, unable to speak. Then he yelled:

HAIR!

HAIR!

HAIR!!?

When he stopped yelling, he said: 'Why have I suddenly sprouted all this hair? I've been bald for years and tried all kinds of remedies, none of which worked, until now that is.'

He stood for a moment in silence, then clapped one hand to his head, exclaiming: 'I know what it was! It was that widow who came to beg me to find her son a job. She started complaining about how poor she was, and I started complaining about my lack of hair.

She said: "I have no money!"

And I responded: "Well, I have no hair!"

And then she said she would send me a remedy that would make my hair grow. And the following day, she sent me a bottle of the stuff. I rubbed it into my scalp, and my hair grew! I must thank her! I must find a job for her son! Now!'

And the Very Rich Man excitedly snatched up the phone and dialled a number.

The widow answered and, after the usual exchange of niceties, the Very Rich Man said: 'I am beside myself with gratitude, Madam. I kneel at your feet and kiss your hands. I have hair again, imagine that! I might even end up with ringlets! Possibly blond ringlets! My greatest ambitions in life were always to be rich and blond. So far, I've only managed to be rich. Now, thanks to you, I'm going to be blond as well! I want to thank you. I want to speak to your son!'

The widow's son came on the phone, and the Very Rich Man said: 'I have a job for you. A magnificent job, perfect, ideal. You'll get paid handsomely each month simply for turning up twice a week. You don't even have to do anything. It's a very important job. They offered it to me, but now I'm giving it to you!'

On hearing this, Oriana thought: 'Phew! At last I've managed to do some good in this house. I can go now!'

And she left by the window.

The Fish

It was a wonderfully fresh day. The breeze was dancing with the grass in the fields. You could hear the birds singing. The air seemed to be made of gold dust.

Oriana set off through the forest, running, dancing and flying until she reached the river. It was a very small, clear river, almost a stream really, and on its banks grew clover, poppies and daisies. Oriana sat down among the grass and the flowers to watch the water flowing by. Then she heard a voice calling to her: 'Oriana, Oriana.'

She turned and saw a fish floundering about on the sand.

'Save me, Oriana,' cried the fish. 'I leapt up to catch a fly and landed on the bank.'

Oriana picked up the fish and put him back in the water.

'Thank you, thank you,' said the fish, bowing repeatedly. 'You saved my life, and the life of a fish is such a delightful one. Thank you, Oriana. If ever you need anything, remember, you only have to ask.'

'Thank you,' said Oriana, 'but I don't need anything just now.'

'Remember my promise, though. I will never forget that I owe you my life. Ask me anything you like. Without you I would have suffocated to death among the clover and the daisies. I'm eternally grateful.'

'Thank you,' said Oriana.

'Goodbye, Oriana. I have to go now, but if ever you need me, just come down to the river and call for me.'

After more deep bows, the fish took his leave.

Oriana looked at the fish as he swam away, and she smiled, because, although he was a very small fish, he had a very self-important air.

And as she was looking at him, she saw her own face reflected in the water. The reflection rose up from the bottom of the stream and came to meet her with a smile on its red lips. And Oriana saw her eyes blue as sapphires, her hair golden as wheat, her skin white as lilies and her wings the colour of the pale, shining air.

'How pretty I am,' she said. 'Really lovely. It had never occurred to me before. I had never thought to look at myself. How large my eyes are, how delicate my nose, how golden my hair! My eyes shine like blue stars, my neck is long and slender. How strange life is! If it hadn't been for that fish jumping out of the water to catch a fly, I would never have seen myself. The trees, the animals and the flowers saw me and knew I was pretty. I was the only one who didn't see that!'

Oriana was amazed at her discovery. Leaning over the water, she couldn't stop gazing at her own face. The hours passed, and she continued to talk to her reflection until the sun set, night fell, the river grew dark, and she could no longer see her own image. She stood up and remained there for some time, thinking. Then she looked around her and said: 'Goodness, it's dark already. How quickly time passes!'

Then she remembered it was time to visit her friend the Poet, who, because he was different from other grown-ups, was the only one to whom Oriana was visible.

The Poet lived in the depths of the forest, in a very tall, very ancient tower, all overgrown with ivy, wisteria and roses. Oriana flew above the trees through the early blue of the night, and even though the door of the tower was open, she instead flew in through the window on the breeze. The climbing roses trembled and danced when she arrived.

'You're late,' said the Poet.

'I was sitting by the river looking at my reflection,' Oriana said. 'I'm late because I became spellbound by my own beauty.'

'Oriana,' said the Poet, 'please put a spell on the night.'

Then Oriana touched the night with her magic wand, and the night fell under her spell.

And the Poet said: 'You bring me much more than just beauty. There are many pretty girls in the world, but only you, Fairy Oriana, can put a spell on the night.'

Then Oriana perched by the window and told marvellous tales about the horses of the wind, the cave of the dragons and the rings of Saturn. The Poet read his poems to her, and they were as pale and bright as stars. Then the Poet and Oriana both fell silent while the Moon rose in the sky, until a distant bell brought them the sound of midnight, and Oriana and the Poet said goodbye.

The following morning, Oriana accompanied the old lady to the city, but on their return, she flew straight to the river. She knelt on the bank and leaned over the water. Her reflection appeared on the surface, all gilded by the sun.

'How pretty I am!' said Oriana. 'I'm even prettier today than I was yesterday. Can I really be as pretty as I am in my reflection?'

Oriana looked at other places along the river, where the trees were reflected in the water. And it seemed to her that the trees' reflections were prettier than the trees themselves.

'Perhaps,' she thought, 'my reflection is prettier than me! How can I ever be sure?'

Then she remembered the fish and called to him: 'Fish, fish, where are you, my friend?'

The fish duly appeared and said: 'Good morning, Oriana. Here I am.'

'Fish,' said Oriana, 'I need you. I want to know if my reflection in the river is prettier than I am.'

'Nothing in the world is as pretty as you,' said the fish. 'You are far prettier than your reflection. Your eyes are brighter, your hair more golden, your lips redder.'

'Do you really think so?'

And she sat there, deep in thought.

Suddenly, she had an idea: 'I'll go and see what the mirror says.'

She said goodbye to the fish, and, swift as an arrow, hurried back to the Very Rich Man's house. The same window stood open, and there was no one in the room.

Oriana entered, said good morning to all the

various furnishings and stood in front of the mirror: 'Mirror,' she said, 'take a good look at me and show me as I really am. I saw my reflection in the river and thought I was lovely, but I'm afraid the river might have made me look prettier than I am, the way it does with the trees and the countryside. Show me exactly what I look like so that I can see if what the fish said is true, and whether I really am even prettier than my reflection in the river.'

'Oriana,' said the mirror, 'I am, as you are aware, a very ancient mirror. Over the centuries, many pretty girls have stood before me to see what they look like and to find out if there is anyone in the world prettier than them. Take a good look at yourself. You *are* very pretty, but there is something even prettier than you.'

'What's that?' asked Oriana eagerly.

'A smooth, bare, white wall.'

'Oh, not that wall again!' said Oriana, momentarily downcast.

But then she looked at herself in the mirror for a long time and said: 'I think I'm pretty.'

'Good,' said the mirror. 'But you can't imagine the number of other girls who, over the centuries, have gazed into my glass eyes and said: "I think I'm pretty".'

'Goodbye then,' said Oriana, slightly annoyed.

'No, don't go just yet. I'd like to ask you something.'

'What's that?'

'Can you take away the Very Rich Man's hair?'

'Why would I do something so cruel?'

'Because he spends all day standing in front of me, saying "What lovely hair." And I can't bear to look at him a moment longer.'

'In this house,' sighed Oriana, 'nothing ever turns out well.'

And with that she left.

Once outside, she thought: 'I'm never going back to that house. The mirror made fun of me. This is a household that has absolutely everything and yet nothing ever turns out right.'

And she went back to the river.

She sat at the water's edge, and the fish appeared.

'Fish,' said Oriana, 'I saw myself in the mirror belonging to the Very Rich Man, and I thought I looked very pretty, as pretty as my reflection in the river. But the mirror told me that there was a smooth, bare, white wall that was even prettier than me!'

'Mirrors are great dreamers, and are always imagining what they can't see. You're much prettier than a wall. I've never seen anyone as pretty as you, but it's a shame about your hair.'

'My hair?' said Oriana anxiously.

'Yes, you need to change your hair,' said the fish. 'I'll teach you.'

And the fish began to teach her.

'Make a side parting, comb your curls back and bring that wavy bit on the right further forward and the wavy bit on the left further back and leave some curls covering your neck.'

Oriana did everything the fish said, but still he wasn't satisfied. He told her to undo what she had done and start all over again. Oriana combed and uncombed waves and curls, until dusk fell.

'That's better,' said the fish. 'But tomorrow we'll try another style.'

'I'll see you tomorrow, then,' said Oriana.

And she walked slowly, pensively, back through the forest.

It was almost night when she reached the Poet's tower. She sat down on the windowsill and asked: 'Do I look different to you?'

'No,' said the Poet. 'You look exactly the same.'

'But I've changed my hairstyle.'

'I didn't notice.'

Oriana fell silent, disappointed with his response. The Poet said: 'Oriana, fill the air with music.'

Oriana waved her magic wand, and the air filled with music.

It was a full moon, and the moonlight illuminated everything. The air smelled of honeysuckle and roses.

'Oriana,' said the Poet, 'dance the dance of the night.'

And on tiptoes in the air, Oriana began to dance the 'Dance of the Night of Spring Moonlight'.

She danced the way the flowers dance in the wind, and her arms were like the flowing rivers.

The Poet sat down on the windowsill to watch her, and out from the depths of the forest came the deer, the rabbits, the birds and the butterflies to watch her dance.

Until the wind brought the distant sound of the twelve strokes of midnight, and Oriana said goodbye to the Poet and vanished.

The following morning, having, as usual, accompanied the old lady to the city, Oriana raced back to kneel by the river, where the fish was waiting for her. They immediately began to try out different hairstyles. The fish told her to make a garland of flowers for her head. Oriana spent the morning picking flowers, looking at her reflection and listening to the fish's flattering remarks. She forgot to go to the miller's house and to the woodman's house. She forgot to take care of the animals. She forgot to water the flowers. But that night, she went to visit the Poet.

And from then on, Oriana gradually abandoned all the people, animals and plants that lived in the forest. One day, she even abandoned the Poet. And this was because, one afternoon, the fish said to her: 'You're very pretty seen by the light of the Sun, but I bet you'd be even prettier at night, by the light of a flame.'

And that night, instead of visiting the Poet, Oriana filled the river bank with fireflies and will-o'-the-wisps and spent the whole night gazing at herself in the water.

It was a marvellous night, like an extraordinary, fantastical party in the middle of the dark, silent forest.

The will-o'-the-wisps and the fireflies were like tiny stars, and Oriana saw herself in the water, surrounded by lights, flames and shadows, her eyes shining, her hair gleaming, her head crowned with lilies, and her wings transparent.

And after that, she never again went to visit the Poet. She forgot all her friends. The only person she continued to visit was the old lady, because she felt so sorry for her when she heard her saying that, in days long gone, she had been young and pretty, but now she was old and wrinkled and ugly. That is why, every morning, Oriana lit the fire, put milk in the jug, coffee in the tin, sugar in the sugar bowl, bread and butter in the bread bin, then led her along the road to the city, so that she wouldn't fall into the ravines.

However, as soon as she returned from the city with the old lady, she went straight to the river, to contemplate her own beauty and hear the flattering words of her admirer, the fish.

And all that spring, Oriana adorned herself with garlands and necklaces made of honeysuckle, daisies, narcissi, orange blossom and poppies. Then, in the summer, she adorned herself with carnations, roses and lilies, and, in the autumn, with red vine leaves, dahlias and chrysanthemums.

But when winter came, there were only violets.

And after a while, the fish said: 'I think the colour of the violets really suits your pale skin and your golden hair, but it's been days and days now since you changed your garland. I think you should vary it a bit.'

'But how?' asked Oriana. 'It's winter now, and there are no other flowers in the forest.'

The fish thought for a while, then said: 'You could adorn yourself with pearls.'

'And where would I find pearls?'

'Wait a moment,' said the fish.

And shortly afterwards, he returned with a ring.

'Take this ring,' he said.

Oriana took the ring, and the fish told her: 'Put the ring on your finger and fly to the sea, and when you reach the sea's edge, call for a fish called Solomon, show him the ring and ask him to bring you a thousand pearls from the Oriental Sea.'

Oriana did as he asked.

She flew over forests, mountains, cities and fields until she came to a vast, deserted beach, where the foaming waves broke on the shore.

And she went to the sea's edge and called: 'Solomon, Solomon.'

And a fish with blue-black scales and red eyes appeared and asked: 'Who calls me?'

'It's me, the Fairy Oriana. I bring you this ring.'

'What do you want?'

'I want you to bring me a thousand pearls from the Oriental Sea.'

'Sit on that rock,' said Solomon, 'and wait for me to come back.'

Oriana sat on the rock and waited for seven

days and seven nights.

Now and then, she would remember the old lady, but thought: 'Solomon won't be gone much longer, and the old lady won't even notice my absence. Besides, by now, she knows the road so well that she won't fall into the ravines.'

At dawn after the seventh night, Solomon reappeared, bringing with him a large turtle shell containing a thousand pearls.

'Thank you, Solomon,' said Oriana.

And picking up the turtle shell, she returned to the forest.

The Fairy Queen

As soon as she reached the riverbank, Oriana called out: 'Fish! Here are the pearls, my friend!'

And from the bottom of the river the fish fetched ten strands of silver onto which Oriana threaded the pearls to make ten necklaces.

She wrapped one necklace around her neck, then one around each wrist, then wove the seven remaining necklaces into her hair.

Then she leaned over the water. It was a very clear, bright winter's day, and Oriana could see her reflection more clearly and crisply than ever.

She had never seen herself look so pretty. The soft gleam of pearls encircled her neck, making her skin glow and her hair shine.

'I have never, ever seen anything so beautiful! she exclaimed.

'You look like the sea queen, the moon princess, the pearl goddess,' said the fish.

'I will never again leave this riverbank,' said Oriana. 'I want to spend the rest of my life looking at myself.'

But suddenly Oriana stopped. Perhaps because she heard a silence in the air. Through the silence came a voice, a loud, stern, forthright voice, calling her: 'Oriana!'

Oriana trembled and turned around. Beside her, hovering in the air, was the Fairy Queen.

And the loud, stern, forthright voice spoke once again: 'Oriana, what were you doing?'

Turning pale, Oriana replied: 'I was looking at myself.'

'And what about your promise?'

Oriana bowed her head and did not reply.

'Oriana,' said the voice, 'you have broken your promise and abandoned the forest. You have abandoned the people and the animals and plants. The children were afraid and you weren't there to comfort them, the poor were hungry and you didn't give them food, the birds fell from their nests and you didn't catch them, the Poet waited for you until the twelve strokes of midnight and you did not appear. You abandoned the woodman, the miller and the Poet. You even abandoned the old lady. You did not keep your promise. For a whole spring, summer and autumn you spent the days and nights gazing into a river, being flattered by a fish, and in love with yourself. Because of this, Oriana, you will no longer have wings and you will lose your magic wand.'

And as she said this, the Fairy Queen waved her hand in the air. That very instant, Oriana watched as her wings, like leaves falling from the trees in autumn, fell from her shoulders and then shrivelled up, as dry and lifeless as two crumpled pieces of paper. The wind blew and carried them away. Oriana ran after them, but she could no longer fly and the wings disappeared off into the distance. Then she watched her magic wand break into little pieces and crumble into dust that fell to the ground. Oriana knelt on the ground, trying to scoop up the dust. But the dust was already mixed in with the earth and so all that Oriana managed to scoop up was earth.

And the loud, stern, forthright voice called out once again: 'Oriana!'

Oriana stood up and, with tears streaming down her face and with her hands full of earth, she begged the Fairy Queen: 'Please give me back my wings! Please give me back my magic wand! Forgive my vanity. I know I broke my promise, I know I abandoned the people, animals and plants of the forest. The fish made me vain with his flattery. I looked at my own image for so long that I forgot everything else. But please, give me back my wings. I want to be like I was before. I want to help the people, animals and plants once again. But I cannot be a fairy without my wings and magic wand. I need wings to fly to whoever calls me, and I need my magic wand to be able to help those who need me.'

However, the loud, stern, forthright voice of the Fairy Queen replied: 'Go into the forest and see the harm you have done. See what has happened to the people, animals and plants you abandoned. While you were looking at yourself, you forgot about everyone else. You will only have your wings again once you have undone all the harm you caused. You will only have your wings again when you forget about yourself and start thinking about others.'

And as soon as she had said these words, the Fairy Queen vanished.

Oriana was alone on the riverbank, with tears streaming down her face and her hands full of earth.

She knelt by the river to wash her hands. But when she saw her reflection in the water without her wings, she began to cry and say: 'Wings, wings, oh, my poor wings! How ugly a fairy looks without wings! How ridiculous a fairy is without wings! No one will believe that I'm a fairy. They'll think I'm just a pretty little girl. But I don't want to be just a pretty little girl. I want to be a fairy.'

Oriana felt very sad and very alone.

She remembered the fish and thought: 'I'm going to ask the fish to help me. He's to blame for all of this.'

And she began to call out: 'Fish, fish, where are you, my friend!'

But the fish did not appear.

Oriana called out again: 'Fish, fish, come and console me! Come and see how sad I am! Come and see what has happened to me!'

But the fish did not appear.

'He must have swum far away,' Oriana thought. 'I'll wait until he returns.'

And she waited and waited, sitting on the

riverbank. But many hours passed and the fish did not appear.

'What a bad friend,' thought Oriana. 'here I am feeling sad and he doesn't even come to console me.'

Then Oriana remembered the old friends she had abandoned. And she remembered what the Fairy Queen had told her: 'Go and see what happened to the people, animals and plants you abandoned.'

So she got up, dried her tears and began to run through the forest.

The Abandoned Forest

Everything was very still and very silent. The forest seemed deserted. No birds sang and not a single flower was to be seen. But there were poisonous toadstools everywhere. Oriana called out: 'Birds, squirrels, deer, rabbits and hares!'

Then she heard something moving in the undergrowth, and a small black snake appeared.

'Good morning,' said the snake.

'Good morning, snake,' replied Oriana. 'Where are all the other animals?'

'They've all gone to the mountains. Ever since the fairy Oriana abandoned them and they had no one to protect them from the hunters' guns, they had to flee far, far away. Only the mice, snakes, ants, mosquitoes and spiders remain.'

'Oh dear!' said Oriana, blushing with shame.

And she asked: 'Do you know who I am?'

'No,' said the snake. 'All I can see is a very pretty little girl.'

'I am not a pretty little girl. I am a fairy. I am Oriana, the fairy.'

'Ah! But how strange! Where are your wings? I've never seen a fairy without wings.'

'I don't have wings at the moment, but in a few days I will have them back again. I can't tell you the whole story.'

'Well, I've never seen you, since I'm always slithering around in the earth, but I have heard about you.'

'Have you? What did they say about me?'

'They told me that you used to be very good and took care of the forest, but one day you abandoned all your friends because you fell in love with a fish.'

'That's a lie,' said Oriana angrily. 'I never fell in love with the fish. What a silly story!'

'Well then, just so you know, that's what I've heard. They even say that you would spend hours and hours and hours bent over the river combing your hair and adorning yourself with flowers just so the fish would tell you how beautiful you were.'

'But I never fell in love with the fish. I spent hours beside the river because I liked looking at my reflection.'

'Maybe you're right. But the fish told the other fish, who told the birds, who told the rabbits, who told the snakes, that you were madly in love with him and that you were only prettifying yourself like that so that he would find you beautiful."

Oriana was most indignant. She felt ridiculous. She looked at the snake and said: 'That is a very silly lie. A fairy cannot fall in love with a fish. That story is pure gossip. It's the typical nasty gossip you'd expect from a snake.'

Oriana turned her back and set off again, but as she left, she heard the evil hissing laughter of the snake: 'SSSSSSSSSS!'

After walking a long, long way, she came to the miller's house. The door was open. Inside everything was a complete mess: the drawers and cupboards were all open and empty, the floor and furniture covered in dust, and there were broken things lying everywhere. The house looked as if it had been abandoned a long time ago. The fire was out and the rooms were full of cobwebs. Oriana took a broom and a rag and began to sweep and clean the house. Then she heard a sound and a voice calling her: 'Oriana!'

It was a mouse.

'Oriana, there's no point tidying the house. No one lives here any more except me. The miller, the miller's wife and their children have gone to live in the city.'

'Oh! But why?' asked Oriana.

'One day, one of their youngest children disappeared, the four-year-old with dark curly hair. For nine days, the miller and his wife searched for him everywhere in the forest, but they didn't find him and at the end of the nine days the miller said: "Our son is lost in the forest, or else he's been eaten by wolves, or has fallen into the river and drowned and been carried far away. There's no point in looking for him any more. Let's leave the forest before any more disasters occur."

"For a long time now, I had a sense that something bad was going to happen," said the miller's wife. "Lately, everything's been going wrong for me. When I come home, I find everything in a mess. My children are always falling into the river and coming home dirty and tattered and covered in scratches. Let's leave the forest immediately."

'After this conversation, the miller and his wife packed their bags, put everything on a cart and went off to the city with their children. That's why there's no point in you tidying the house.'

'It's all my fault,' sighed Oriana. 'I was the one who abandoned them. The miller's children fell in the river and came home dirty, tattered and scratched because I didn't take care of them. And worst of all, one of them was lost completely. How can I ever undo the harm I have done?'

As she said this, Oriana began to weep beside the cold hearth.

'Yes, it is very sad indeed,' said the mouse. 'And it really was all your fault.'

Oriana picked up the broom and said: 'Well, despite everything, I'm going to finish tidying and cleaning the house.'

When she had finished cleaning, the fairy said goodbye to the mouse and went back out into the forest. The path was stony and bruised her feet, and the gorse and brambles pricked her. When Oriana had wings, she simply flew over the rough bits of the path, and only set her feet on the ground where it was covered in moss, soft grass or fine sand.

'How difficult people's lives are,' she thought. 'They don't have wings to fly over bad things.'

Oriana continued walking and came to the woodman's cabin. There, too, the fire was out and the floor covered in dust.

The bed, table and benches had all gone. Oriana knelt by the empty fireplace and wept. Then she heard a voice saying: 'Oriana, what happened to your wings?'

It was an ant.

'The Fairy Queen took my wings away because I broke the promise I'd made to her.'

'Quite right too, because you forgot your friends and abandoned them. See what happened here in this cabin. The woodman and his wife were very poor, but you used to come here every morning with three small white stones, and you turned the stones into bread, clothing and coins. Then one morning you didn't come. And from that day on there was only cold, hunger and poverty in this cabin. Then there came a day when the woodman said to his wife: "We can't go on living in such poverty. Let's go to the city to find work."

And they made a bundle of their few ragged clothes, carried their few sticks of furniture on their backs, and, holding their son by the hand, they left for the city. They did so very sadly, and they wept a lot as they said farewell to this cabin where they had been so happy, in the days when you used to visit them daily with those three white stones.

'Oh, ant,' said Oriana, sobbing, 'how shall I ever undo all the harm I have done? Only now do I understand how important my promise was. Only now do I understand how much the forest needs me.'

'I don't know how to advise you,' replied the ant. 'But since you do truly repent of having abandoned us, and since you want to come back and help the people, animals and plants, then do something for me.'

'What?' asked Oriana, wiping away her tears.

'Pick up a white stone and turn it into a sugar lump.'

'Oh dear!' Said Oriana. 'I don't have my magic wand any more. I can't do what you ask me. I'm no use even to an ant.'

'Well then, if you can't help me, farewell, Oriana. I have lots of things to do.'

And the ant hurried busily away.

Oriana sighed, stood up and left the cabin.

Outside, it was already getting dark. The fairy set off for the Poet's tower. The tower was far away and the path was very overgrown and full of stones and thorns that cut her feet. No bird sang, no rabbit ran, and no deer appeared with its majestic air and dewy eyes. Silence, neglect and solitude reigned. Night had already fallen when Oriana reached the tower. Her feet were bleeding and her heart was heavy.

The door of the tower was open. Oriana entered and went up the stairs, thinking: 'The Poet will comfort me, and tell me what I should do. He'll let me rest my head on his shoulder and weep and weep until my loneliness is gone.'

Oriana opened the door of the Poet's bedroom. But the room was empty.

The sheaves of paper that had once covered the furniture and the floor had gone. But the fireplace was filled with the ashes of burned papers. The wind, coming in through the open window, was blowing the ash everywhere. Everything was covered in ash.

Oriana picked her way across the room and her cut and bloodied feet left red footprints in the soft, white ash. She knelt in front of the fireplace and, weeping bitterly, she said: 'I came looking for my friend and didn't find him. Oh, how can I undo the harm I have done? I have ruined the happiness of people, animals and things. I forgot my promise and I broke my word. Now I find only unlit fires, empty homes and ash.'

Then a spider dropped down from the ceiling, suspended on its shining thread, and asked her: 'Are you the fairy Oriana?'

'I know I am Oriana, but I don't know if I am still a fairy. I broke my promise and the Queen of the Fairies has punished me: the wind has taken away my wings, and my magic wand has turned to dust.'

'Quite right too,' said the spider, 'because you abandoned your friends. I will tell you what happened in this house. One night, you did not come. The following day, as night fell, the Poet sat by the window waiting for you. And whenever a leaf stirred, a twig snapped, or the breeze made the tall grasses dance, he would say: "It's Oriana!" But it wasn't you. You never came back. He waited night after endless night. Not reading, not writing, not doing anything at all.

'He paced around the room, muttering to himself. Until one night, just before dawn, as the cockerel began to crow, he said: "Oriana lied. She told me: 'I will never leave you.' But I have waited and waited. The nights have passed slowly, one by one. Oriana isn't coming back.

"The spell is broken. I want to go to the city and

be the same as other men.

"I want to become the same as other men who don't believe in magic and who don't write poems. I'm going to burn all my books and all my papers."

After he said this, he made a big fire in the hearth with all the books and papers on which he had written his poems.

'He sat down to watch the fire burn, and the light from the flames danced on his pale, sad face. When everything had been reduced to ash, he stood up and left for the city. I watched him disappear into the cold light of morning.'

'It was all my fault,' said Oriana. 'How can I make his poems rise from the ashes? What should I do to rekindle my dear friend's happiness and affections? Oh, how that fish deluded and deceived me with his empty compliments! I just want to undo all the harm I have done. I will go to the city and find my human friends. Then I will go to the mountains and find my animal friends.'

Oriana stood up, said goodbye to the spider and left for the city. She went through the forest once again, cutting her feet on the stones and getting scratched by brambles. She followed the path past the deep ravines and, at midday, she came to the city.

The City

The streets were full of people, and Oriana felt very lost and very confused amid all the houses, noise and commotion. She looked all around for someone who could help her. But she saw only strangers who passed by without even seeing her.

She decided to ask the traffic policeman.

'Excuse me, Mr Policeman, do you know a miller who came from the forest and has eleven children?'

'There are a million people in this city, and I don't know any millers. Move on, miss, you're blocking the traffic!'

Oriana moved on, pushed and jostled by the crowd.

Then she asked a newspaper seller: 'Please sir, could you tell me where the miller lives, the one who came from the forest and has eleven children?'

'There are so many people living in this city! How would I know where this miller of yours lives? Get out of my way!'

Oriana then went into a hat shop and the shopkeeper came bustling towards her.

Oriana asked her: 'Do you know a miller who came from the forest and has eleven children?'

'No, I don't. But I have a lovely hat here that could have been made for you. Sit down in front of the mirror and see how pretty you look in it.'

But Oriana remembered the fish and fled the shop.

Then she saw a man sitting outside a bar drinking a beer, and asked him: 'Do you know a miller who came from the forest and has many children?'

'I don't know any miller but I'd like to get to know you, because I've never seen such a pretty girl here in the city.'

Again Oriana remembered the fish's compliments and fled, terrified.

And she continued to ask all kinds of different people about the miller, but no one could help her. After traipsing along many streets full of shops, cars and people, she found herself in a very poor neighbourhood on the other side of the city. The streets were dark, narrow and dirty. So dark, so narrow and so dirty that even the sun seemed to shine less brightly there.

'What a sad place!' thought Oriana.

A cat passed.

'Hello, cat,' said Oriana. 'Do you know where the miller lives, the one who came from the forest and has eleven children?'

'Yes, I do,' said the cat. 'Follow me.'

They crossed two streets and went into number 9537. They went up to the fourth floor and knocked on the door.

The miller's wife opened the door.

'Good afternoon,' said Oriana. 'I am the fairy Oriana and I have come from the forest to find you.'

'How very odd,' said the miller's wife. 'Where are your wings?'

Oriana told the woman her story and asked her to return to the forest.

'From now on,' said Oriana, 'I will once again look after your children and tidy your house.'

But the miller's wife didn't believe her.

'I don't believe in fairies. I'll only believe in your promises, and I'll only go back to the forest if you bring me back the son I lost.'

And with these words she shut the door.

Oriana felt terribly sad. She turned to the cat and said: 'No one believes in me. I am so, so tired! Tell me something: do you know where the woodman lives, the one who came from the forest? Maybe he will believe in me.'

'No, I don't know him,' said the cat.

So they said goodbye.

Once again Oriana wandered through the streets

alone, asking questions that no one could answer.

Until she met a stray dog.

'Tell me, dog, do you know where the woodman lives, the one who came from the forest with his wife and son?'

'Yes, I do,' said the dog. 'Follow me.'

Oriana followed the dog to a really poor part of the city. The houses were made of tin, the women were pale and dishevelled, the men were unshaven and wore tattered clothes. The children were playing in the mud.

'Over there,' said the dog, pointing to a tumbledown shack.

Oriana peered into the shack.

The woodman's wife was sitting on the floor, her son sleeping in her lap. Both of them were so pale and thin that Oriana scarcely recognized them. There was no bed, no mattress, not even a bench or, for that matter, any furniture at all. The only thing was a pile of rags in a corner.

Oriana felt her eyes fill with tears. She felt a lump in her throat and a terrible weight on her shoulders, as if she had wings of lead. Through her tears, she said to the woodman's wife: 'I am the fairy Oriana who abandoned you. It's my fault you've fallen on such hard times. Please forgive me for the harm I've caused you and help me to put it right.'

'What harm have you done to me?' asked the woman. 'I've never seen you before in my life.'

Oriana told her everything. The woman replied: 'I always thought there must be a fairy in the forest. But why did you abandon us? Let me tell you what happened to us: When we arrived in the city, my husband got a job down at the docks. But his wages were very low. We rented a room, but after a while we couldn't pay the rent and the landlord threw us out and kept our furniture. Then we found this shack and used our rags to make a bed on the floor. Winter came and we couldn't sleep because of the wind and rain. We put our son's body between ours so that the rain wouldn't soak him and the wind wouldn't freeze him. One day, our son got sick and wouldn't stop coughing. And during the night, the heat of our bodies wasn't enough to warm him. The doctor came, gave him some medicine and said: "He needs two warm blankets." The next day, after work, my husband went begging for money from door to door throughout the city. But he only got six coins, and the blankets cost fifty. The next day he passed by a shop that was selling blankets. He was a good, honest man, but our son was dying of cold. So he stole two blankets. But the shopkeeper called the police and they chased him, shouting: "Thief! Thief! Catch him!"

'They caught him and put him in jail. I went to the door of the jail to ask for him, with my son in my arms. But they sent me away and said that the father of my son was a thief. So here I am, and there is nothing, absolutely nothing I can do. Since you are a fairy, please help us.'

'What a terrible, terrible thing I've done,' said Oriana. 'When I sat by the river looking at my reflection, I would see my hair, my face, and my long, slender neck. And the harm I was doing seemed good and beautiful to me. But now I can see that the harm I was doing has resulted in empty houses, unlit fires, hunger, cold, tears and jail.'

'Help me,' asked the woodman's wife.

'Come back to the forest with me,' said Oriana. 'I promise that from this day forth I will never again abandon you.'

'I will only go with you if you first fetch my husband from prison. I can't go without him.'

'Then wait for me,' said Oriana. 'I'll go and fetch your husband.'

Oriana headed back out into the city. She walked and walked, until she came to the door of the jail. It was a sad, dark door, covered in damp stains.

'Good afternoon,' she said to the guard. 'Is this where the woodman is being held, the one who stole two woollen blankets?'

'Yes, it is,' said the guard.

'Please will you release him. He's my friend and he isn't a thief. I know that he isn't a thief.'

'He stole,' said the guard. 'That makes him a thief.'

'He stole because his son was dying of cold. That's why he isn't a thief.'

'The law says he's a thief,' replied the guard.

'Don't keep saying he's a thief,' said Oriana.

'You're insulting the authorities. I'll have you locked up for that,' said the guard.

And he called out: 'Bring two guards to arrest this girl!'

When Oriana heard this, she fled. And no one could catch her because, even though she had no wings, she was still a fairy and so could still run much faster than ordinary human beings.

Oriana began wandering the streets again. She was so distraught that she began talking to herself out loud. People laughed at her, saying: 'She's crazy, talking to herself like that.'

Oriana fled in shame.

But there were other people who said: 'What a

pretty little girl! A girl as pretty as that has never set foot in the streets of this city. She's like a lily or a star.'

When she heard this, Oriana fled even further, because she remembered the fish's flattery.

Night began to fall. The sun went out and the lights of the city came on. There were blue lights, green lights, white lights, yellow lights, purple lights and red lights. The pavements of the city gleamed black.

Oriana set out to find the Poet.

She looked for him in the streets, squares and public gardens. She looked for him in the cafés, cake shops, terraces and taverns. She looked for him at the viewpoints overlooking the city, at the tram stops and outside the cinemas. She kept on looking until the lights of the city slowly went out one by one. By the time the first cockerel began to crow just before dawn, there was only one house left with its light on.

'That's where he is,' said Oriana.

She walked towards the light. She came to a wide street lined by tall houses. Oriana had already passed by there that same afternoon, when the street had been full of hustle and bustle, noise and cars. Now everything was still and silent. The doors and shutters were closed, except for one door, the source of the light she had seen.

Oriana peeked in and saw a large room with lots of small tables topped with cold, white marble. It was a café that was full of people during the day. Now, there was hardly anyone there, just one sleepy waiter leaning on the counter, four men sitting sombrely around a table to the right of the entrance, and, there at the back, alone, before an empty glass, was the Poet. Oriana silently crossed the room and sat down in front of him. The Poet was so lost in his thoughts that he didn't even notice her. His eyes were gazing blindly into the distance. The fairy tapped him gently on the hand, and said: 'It's me. I am the fairy Oriana. I've come back!'

'Oriana!' he said, smiling.

He sat there speechless for a moment. But then his smile faded and his face became sad and hard. He asked: 'Where are your wings?'

'I don't have wings any more,' replied Oriana, hanging her head.

'Where's your magic wand?'

'I lost it,' said Oriana.

'If you are Oriana, put a spell on the night.'

'I can't.'

Then the Poet said to her, almost yelling: 'You

aren't Oriana. Your face is the same as Oriana's, but you're lying because you don't have wings and you can't put a spell on the night. You're not Oriana. The spell has been broken. Oriana lives in the forest with the trees, the wind and the flowers. There is no Oriana here. Go away. Right now.'

He was talking louder and louder. People began to stare at them. Oriana covered her face with her hands. And the Poet shouted: 'Get away from me!'

Oriana stood up and, hiding her face, ran out of the café. She heard the waiters and the four men laughing as she passed them. She fled out into the street and their laughter and mockery followed her.

And Oriana went back to the forest.

The Tree and the Animals

Day was dawning when she reached the forest. Everything was white with mist. It was time for the birds to wake up and start to sing. But the birds had flown away to the mountains and no one sang.

'Such silence! Such terrible silence!' whispered Oriana. 'All my bird friends have flown away, leaving me all alone. And oh, how weary I am! I don't know where to go, and I can barely take another step.'

As she said this, Oriana leaned her head against a tree trunk and began to cry.

The trunk was strong and rough, and almost black. Oriana wrapped her arms around it and pressed her face against its rugged bark. Then the tree bent down and picked her up in its branches, cradling her. It covered her with its foliage and lay two leaves over her eyes. Oriana drifted off to sleep.

It was late morning when she awoke. A thousand rays of sunshine pierced the forest. Oriana could see the blue sky through the green leaves above. She stretched and took a deep breath of all the earthy smells. She was filled with happiness to see such beauty.

'What a beautiful morning!' she said aloud.

But suddenly she remembered the previous day. She remembered the woodman, the miller's wife, and the Poet.

She thought to herself: 'I have to find a solution. There must be a solution, there must be. But what should I do?'

Sitting up with her elbows on her knees and resting her chin on her hands, Oriana began to think. Until suddenly she exclaimed: 'I will go and find the miller's son. The animals who went to the mountains must know where he is. I'll ask them to tell me how to find him. And I'll also ask them to come with me to the city and help me free the woodman. And perhaps the fox, who is so intelligent, will manage to convince the Poet that I *am* a fairy.'

Aglow with her new idea, Oriana danced a little jig.

Then she turned back towards the tree and said: 'Thank you, tree. Even though I no longer have my wings, you saw that I was a fairy. When I came to you, I was sad and weary, but you covered me with your leaves and gave me your peace. Now I am going to look for the miller's son. Yesterday I was weeping and thinking that there was no remedy for my sadness. And you covered my eyes with your leaves and while I slept, my sadness melted away. This morning is so wonderfully green and blue! And I am so happy because I'm sure there is a solution!'

Oriana said goodbye to the tree and set off towards the mountains.

The mountains were far away and shimmered blue on the horizon.

Oriana walked and walked.

And she was thinking: 'How difficult the lives of humans are, and all because they have no wings!'

And she walked and walked and walked.

At sunset, the mountains turned dark against the red sky.

Then night came, and the moonlight fell softly over the fields.

Oriana looked around for a tree where she could sleep, because fairies can only sleep in trees.

She found a pine tree.

During the night, the pine tree whispered: 'When the wind blows, I imagine that I'm a mast.'

First thing the next morning, Oriana set off again.

She reached the top of the mountain and summoned all the animals. She told them: 'I am the fairy Oriana.'

And they asked: 'But where are your wings and your magic wand?'

Oriana told them her story and asked: 'Do you know where the miller's son is?'

'He's here,' said the deer, appearing behind a rocky outcrop with the miller's son on his back.

'Give him to me,' said Oriana. 'I want to take him to his mother.'

'A fairy without wings,' said the deer, 'is a very strange thing. I can't hand over a child to you, because a child is a sacred thing. I can't hand over a child to someone who simply says she's a fairy, but can't show me her wings.'

'I am a fairy,' said Oriana, 'but I can't prove that I am.'

'Then provide us with witnesses,' said the rabbit.

'In any case,' said the fox, 'we can't trust her. On the one hand, she doesn't have wings and so doesn't look like a fairy. On the other hand, even if she is the fairy Oriana, we can't trust her, because the fairy Oriana abandoned us, broke her promise and her word.'

'I broke my promise, but I am very sorry,' said Oriana. 'I've been crying for three days now.'

'Bring us a witness,' said the deer.

'The fish knows everything,' said the fairy. 'It's his fault that I forgot all about the people, animals and plants that live in the forest. He saw the Fairy Queen raise her hand in the air and heard her saying that I was going to lose my wings. He watched the wind take away my wings!'

'If the fish says that he saw your wings disappear, carried away by the wind, that it was the Fairy Queen who punished you, and that you are the fairy Oriana, then we will believe you,' said the porcupine.

'And if everyone believes you,' said the deer, 'I

will give you the miller's son to take to his mother.'

'I will go and find the fish,' said Oriana. 'Tomorrow at midday, come and meet me at the riverbank.'

'Tomorrow,' said all the animals, 'we will meet you at the riverbank.'

'Until tomorrow, then,' said Oriana.

And she set off once again.

She walked, and she walked, and she walked.

The following day, just as day was breaking, Oriana leaned over the river, and called: 'Fish, fish, my dear friend fish!'

The fish appeared.

'Good morning, Oriana,' he said, looking somewhat out of sorts. 'Your hair's all over the place.'

'I don't have time to brush my hair,' said Oriana. 'There are much more important things than having neat hair. I have to save all the people, animals and plants that live in the forest. I have to undo the harm I have done. I saw the sadness of the miller's wife, and the poverty in which the woodman lives, and the loneliness of the Poet. I want to make everything good again. I want to help other people. Please tell the animals that you know I'm a fairy.'

'Oriana,' replied the fish, 'I am your very good

friend, but I really cannot disobey the Fairy Queen. The Fairy Queen is very angry with you because you behaved very badly.'

'It was your fault,' said Oriana.

'Excuse me, but it was not my fault,' said the fish. 'I didn't know you had made a promise to look after the people, animals and plants that live in the forest. It's nothing to do with me.'

'There's no point in us arguing,' said Oriana. 'I just want to ask one thing of you: the animals won't believe I'm a fairy because I don't have wings. They say that fairies always have wings. I want you to tell them that you saw the Fairy Queen take my wings away, and that you know I'm the fairy Oriana.'

'Of course I know you're the fairy Oriana,' said the fish. 'But this business with the animals is nothing to do with me.'

'On the day I saved you, fish,' said Oriana, 'you said: "Come to the river whenever you like and call for me. You can ask me for anything you wish." So now I am asking you: tell the animals that I am the fairy Oriana.'

'You know, when someone throws in your face the favour you did for them, she loses the right to our gratitude.'

Oriana turned bright red, struggling to think

of an answer. She wanted to spit at that arrogant, cowardly fish. But she remembered the woodman in prison, the miller's wife not knowing where her son was, and the Poet who no longer believed in fairies. So she told herself to be patient.

'Fish,' she said, 'I'm asking you to tell the animals that I am the fairy Oriana.'

'All right,' said the fish. 'I don't want to seem ungrateful. When the animals get here, call for me.'

'Thank you, thank you, thank you!' said Oriana.

'See you soon then,' said the fish courteously, and with that he vanished.

Oriana sat down to wait for the animals. The sun rose higher and higher in the sky, until it reached midday. And at midday the animals appeared.

They came one by one, very solemnly, in a line. At the front was the wolf, and at the end of the line came the deer, carrying the miller's son on his back.

'Good morning,' said Oriana.

'Good morning,' replied the animals. 'Where is your witness?'

'He's just coming,' said the fairy. 'He's waiting for me to call him.'

And, kneeling at the edge of the river, Oriana called out: 'Fish, fish, my dear friend fish!'

The fish did not appear.

Oriana called once again: 'Fish, fish, my dear friend fish!'

And the fish did not appear.

'So where's the fish?' asked the animals.

'We just need to give him more time,' replied Oriana.

And she called once again: 'Fish, fish, my dear friend fish!'

But the fish still did not appear.

'He's late,' said Oriana.

'Very,' said the pig, who was always very punctual. 'It's gone midday.'

'Let's wait,' said the deer.

They settled down to wait.

From time to time, Oriana would call: 'Fish, fish, my dear friend fish!'

But the fish did not appear.

The sun began to dip down over to the other side of the river.

The animals began to get annoyed. Oriana felt upset and ashamed.

'So is the fish not coming?' asked a rabbit.

'No, he's not coming,' they all concluded.

'Something must have happened to him,' said Oriana. 'He promised he would come and be my witness.'

'But he didn't come,' said the fox.

Oriana began to cry, and said: 'Perhaps someone caught him.'

Some of the animals began to laugh, and others became even more annoyed.

'You said the fish was coming to be your witness, and the fish has not appeared,' shouted the wolf.

'You said you were a fairy and you don't have wings,' grumbled the pig.

'And you don't have a magic wand either,' added the fox.

'You don't have a witness and you're not a fairy,' shouted all the animals together. 'Let's go.'

'I am a fairy,' said Oriana.

'You're lying!' shouted the animals.

'No, I'm not,' said Oriana.

Turning to the deer, tears running down her face, Oriana begged him: 'Give me the miller's son! Believe me: I really am a fairy.'

'No,' replied the deer. 'I don't believe you.'

'Let's go,' said the wolf.

And off they went, leaving Oriana all alone.

Through her tears, she said: 'Cowardly, cowardly fish! You spent day after day telling me I was beautiful and now I call for you and you don't appear. Ungrateful, lying, cowardly fish! I saved your life and now you won't help me. I'm all alone! Who is going to help me?'

Then she heard a noise behind her. She fell silent and listened. A soft, sweet, undulating voice called out:'Oriana.'

Oriana turned and saw, standing beside her, a very pretty fairy, smiling at her. Her eyes shone jet black, her hair hung down like dark blue serpents, and her wings were made of a thousand colours, like the wings of butterflies. In her left hand she was carrying another pair of wings.

'Oriana,' she said, 'would you like to have wings again?'

'Yes, yes, I would,' said Oriana.

'These wings I'm holding in my left hand are for you.'

'For me?' said Oriana, who could scarcely believe what she was hearing.

'Yes.'

'Please, please, give them to me now!' begged Oriana, trembling.

'First, you must make a promise.'

'What promise?' asked Oriana.

Then the dark-haired fairy smiled and said: 'I am the Queen of the Bad Fairies. If you want me to give you these wings, you have to promise that from this day forth you will obey my commands.'

'And what are your commands?' asked Oriana.

'These,' said the Queen of the Bad Fairies, 'are my commands:

Sully the spring waters.
Cast cobwebs on the flowers.
Wither all the seeds germinating in the soil.
Steal the nightingales' voices.
Turn the wine sour.
Steal money from the poor.
Make little children fall over.
Douse the old folks' fires.
Steal the roses' scent.
Torment animals.
Break the spell cast on the world.'

'No! No! No!' said Oriana, recoiling in horror. 'I don't want to do any of those things.'

'If you don't promise to do these things, I won't give you these wings,' said the dark-haired fairy.

'I would rather have no wings.'

'Without wings you cannot be a fairy.'

'I would rather not be a fairy.'

'Think carefully, Oriana: these wings are made of a thousand colours, like the wings of butterflies, and with them you will be able to fly through the air instead of walking with such difficulty, step-by-step, on the ground, cutting your feet on the stones along the way.'

'I would rather be good,' said Oriana. 'I want to be good, even if it means I cannot have wings.'

'I feel really sorry for you, Oriana!' said the bad fairy, laughing. 'You're getting everything the wrong way round: first of all, you lose your wings because some fish flattered you. And now when I bring you a pair of wings just like a butterfly's wings, you don't want them. I pity you, Oriana: you are foolish and silly and you have very bad taste.'

And, chuckling to herself, the dark-haired fairy vanished.

Once again Oriana found herself alone. She began thinking to herself: 'I will never, ever, have wings again. I lost my own blue wings because I did the wrong thing. And I lost those butterfly wings because I didn't want to be bad. Now it's as if I wasn't a fairy at all. No one will ever again believe that I am a fairy. Perhaps even I will forget that I'm a fairy. I will have to live as if I were just like any other girl. I will never again be able to flit and fly over the stony paths. I'll have to pick my way over them, just like other girls. But at least I can be good.

I can go to the city and help others. I must go to the city, because that is where people's lives are most difficult.'

And so Oriana set off for the city.

The Ravine

She walked and walked, and when she was almost halfway there, she saw in the distance a figure coming towards her from the city. The figure was dark and stooped, walking slowly along, leaning on a stick. Oriana realised it was the old lady.

'The poor old lady!' she thought to herself. 'I never went back to help her, and now she's walking alone, almost blind, along this dangerous path beside the ravine. From now on I'm going to go with her every day, just like I used to.'

She began walking faster in order to reach the old lady as quickly as possible.

Then suddenly Oriana let out a cry. She could see that the old lady had lost her bearings and was walking towards the ravine.

'Oh no!' said the fairy. 'She's going to fall into the ravine!'

She cried out: 'Stop! Stop!'

And she began to run.

Oriana was still far away from the old lady, and the old lady was very close to the edge of the ravine, but the old lady was walking very slowly and Oriana was running very fast.

She ran and ran.

And she shouted: 'Stop! Stop!'

But the old lady was deaf and her eyesight very poor, and since she could hardly see or hear anything, she walked very, very slowly.

'I'd already be there if I had wings!' thought Oriana.

And she ran and ran.

At one point, the old lady stopped to rest. She was one step away from the edge. Oriana, who was ten steps away, thought: 'I might just make it!'

But just as Oriana was reaching out her arm to grab her, the old lady took one more step and fell into the ravine.

'Oh no!' shouted Oriana.

And forgetting that she didn't have wings, she jumped into the ravine to save the old lady.

She managed to grab the old lady by the legs and tried to fly, but couldn't. And she remembered that she had no wings.

'We're done for!' she thought.

Beneath her, she saw the deep ravine opening

like an enormous mouth to swallow them up.

'Help, help, help!' screamed the old lady.

And down they fell.

Then suddenly, like a bolt of lightning, the Fairy Queen appeared in the air. She reached out and touched Oriana with her magic wand.

At that very same moment, Oriana stopped falling and hung motionless in the air, still holding on to the old lady.

And the loud, stern, forthright voice said: 'Oriana, today you have kept your promise. You jumped into the ravine to save the old lady, with not a thought for yourself. You were so concerned for your friend that you didn't even think to be afraid because you are the fairy Oriana, to whom the plants, animals and people of the forest were entrusted. It is you who looks after them so that they may live in peace. When you abandoned them, the animals fled to the mountains, the flowers withered and the people went to the city, where they became lost in the maze of streets. But today you kept your promise. I therefore command that a pair of wings will once again spring from your shoulders.'

As she said this, the Fairy Queen waved her right hand in the air.

Suddenly a new pair of wings appeared on

Oriana's shoulders.

'Wings, wings, oh, my wings!' shouted Oriana, trembling with joy.

And giving Oriana her magic wand, the Fairy Queen said to her: 'Take this magic wand, and never again forget your promise!'

As soon as she finished speaking, the Fairy Queen vanished in a flash of light.

Then Oriana flew with the old lady back to the path and, setting her down on the ground, guided her back to the forest.

Dizzy with fright, the old lady looked around her and said: 'Ah, it looks like the fairies have returned!'

But Oriana had already gone. Quick as an arrow, she was flying towards the mountains.

When she got there, she summoned the deer, the wolf, the fox, the porcupine and the rabbits, and asked them to give her the miller's son.

The animals saw that she was a fairy with wings and a magic wand, and so they gave her the child.

Oriana took him in her arms and flew very high above the clouds to the city.

When she spied the street where the miller lived, she came down from the sky and knocked on the door of his house. The door opened, and the miller's wife appeared. She let out a cry when she saw her son in the arms of a fairy.

'Here is the son you lost,' said Oriana.

'Now I can see that you are a fairy,' said the miller's wife. 'Tomorrow we will all go back to the forest.'

Then Oriana went to the jail. Using her wand, she put the guards to sleep, then opened the cell and freed the woodman.

And that same day, the woodman, his wife and their son returned to the forest.

When night came, Oriana went into the café. The waiter was leaning against the bar asleep, and the four men were talking with their backs to the room. At the table at the rear, pale and alone, sat the Poet.

Oriana crossed the room without anyone seeing her. She stopped in front of the Poet and touched him lightly on the hand.

He raised his head and saw her. He saw her wings and her magic wand. And he saw that she was floating in the air, her feet not touching the ground.

'It's me,' she said.

'Now I can see that it's you. Now I can see that you are a fairy. Thank you, Oriana, for coming back.'

Oriana gave her his hand and they left the café

unnoticed. They flew over the city and its maze of neon-lit streets. They flew over squares, avenues and quays, and left the city behind them.

They followed the path along the ravine until they reached the forest.

The full moon shone over the mountains and fields.

When they came to the forest, the Poet asked her: 'Oriana, cast a spell over everything.'

Oriana raised her magic wand, and everything fell under her spell.

Christmas Eve

The Friend

Once upon a time, there was a yellow house with a garden all around it. In the garden grew lime trees, birches, a very ancient cedar, a cherry tree and two plane trees. Joana used to play beneath the cedar tree. She would make little houses out of moss and grass and twigs and lean them against the wide, dark trunk. Then she would imagine the dwarves who - always assuming they existed - might live in those houses. And she planned to make a bigger, more complicated house for the King of the Dwarves.

Joana had no brothers or sisters and so she played alone. Now and then, her two cousins or some other children would come to play with her, and sometimes she was invited to parties, but the children whose houses she went to or who came to her house weren't really friends. They were visitors.

They made fun of her moss houses and found her garden terribly boring.

And Joana was very sad because she didn't know how to play with other children. She only knew how to be alone.

One October morning, though, she found a friend.

Joana was sitting perched on the garden wall, and a boy came walking down the road. His clothes were very old and patched, and his eyes shone like two stars. He was walking slowly along the edge of the pavement, smiling up at the autumn leaves. Joana's heart gave a leap.

'Ah,' she thought. 'He looks like a friend, yes, he's exactly how a friend should look.'

And from her perch on the wall, she said: 'Good morning!'

The boy turned, smiled and said: 'Good morning!'

The two remained silent for a moment, then Joana asked: 'What's your name?'

'Manuel,' said the boy.

'My name's Joana.'

And another light, airy silence passed between them.

In a neighbouring garden a bell rang.

Then the boy said: 'Your garden's really beautiful.'

'Yes, it is, why don't you come in and see for yourself?'

And Joana climbed down from the wall and went and opened the gate.

And together they strolled through the garden. The boy looked at everything. Joana showed him the pond and the goldfish. She showed him the orchard, the orange trees and the vegetable patch. And she called to the dogs so that she could introduce them to him as well. And she showed him the wood stack where a cat was sleeping. And she showed him all the trees and the lawns and the flowers.

'Oh, it's lovely, really lovely,' said the boy gravely.

'And this,' said Joana, 'is the cedar tree. This is where I play.'

And they sat down in the round shade of the cedar.

The morning light encircled the garden. Everything was full of peace and coolness. Occasionally, a yellow seed pod would fall from the lime tree, spinning as it fell.

Joana went to look for pebbles, twigs and moss and, together, she and the boy began building the house for the King of the Dwarves.

They played like this for a long time, until a factory siren sounded in the distance.

'Midday,' said the boy. 'I have to go.'

'Where do you live?'

'On the other side of the pine forest.'

'Is that where your house is?'

'Yes, but it's not really a house.'

'What is it then?'

'My father is in heaven, which is why we're so poor. My mother works all day, but we still don't have enough to be able to afford a house.'

'But where do you sleep at night?'

'The owner of the forest has a hut where he keeps a cow and a donkey. Out of charity, he lets me sleep there too.'

'And where do you play?'

'Oh, I play everywhere. We used to live in the centre of the city, and then I'd play on the pavement and in the gutter. I'd play with empty cans and old newspapers, with bits of rag and pebbles. Now I play in the pine forest and on the road. I play with the grass and the weeds and the animals and the flowers. You can play anywhere.'

'I'm not allowed to leave this garden, so why don't you come back tomorrow and play with me again?'

From then on, every morning, the boy would come walking down the street, and Joana would perch on the wall waiting for him.

She would open the gate, and they would both go and sit in the round shade of the cedar tree. And that was how Joana found a friend.

He was a particularly marvellous friend too. The flowers would turn to look at him when he passed, the light shone more brightly around him, and when Joana brought breadcrumbs from the kitchen, the birds would come and eat them from his hand.

The Party

After many days and many weeks, Christmas came around.

And on Christmas Eve, Joana put on her blue velvet dress and her black patent-leather shoes, and then, at half past seven, with her hair carefully brushed and combed, she left her room and went downstairs.

There she heard voices coming from the big living room: the grown-ups talking. And because Joana knew they had closed the door so as to keep her out, she went into the dining room to see if the glasses were already on the table.

The glasses spent their lives shut up in a big dark wooden cabinet in the corridor. The cabinet was kept locked with a large key, and its two doors were never fully opened. Inside were all kinds of shadows and lights. It was like a cave full of marvels and secrets. Many things were kept locked up inside, things that weren't needed for everyday life, glittering, rather magical things: china cups, bottles, little boxes, goblets and birds made of glass. There was even a dish containing three wax apples and a silver bell in the shape of a little girl. There was also a big Easter egg made of red porcelain and decorated with golden flowers.

Joana had never seen right to the back of the cabinet. She wasn't allowed to open the doors herself, and she only occasionally managed to persuade the maid to let her peer inside.

On party days, the glasses would emerge from that dark shadowy interior. They were clear, transparent, glinting, and they tinkled when carried on a tray. For Joana that tinkling sound was the music of parties.

Joana walked round the table. The glasses were already there, so cold and luminous that they looked more as if they had come from some mountain spring than from the dark depths of a cabinet.

The candles were lit and their flickering light pierced the glass. The table was full of other extraordinary, marvellous things too: glass baubles, golden pinecones and a plant with prickly leaves and red berries.

It was a party. It was Christmas.

Then Joana went out into the garden, because she knew that the stars are different on Christmas Eve.

She opened the door and went down the steps from the verandah. It was very cold, but even the cold seemed to glow. The lime trees, the birches and the cherry trees had all lost their leaves. Their bare branches stood silhouetted in the air like black lace. Only the branches of the cedar tree were still covered in needles.

And very high up, above the trees, was the vast, dark dome of the sky. And in that darkness, the stars sparkled more brightly than anything else. Down below, it was party time, which is why there were so many shining things: candles, glass baubles and crystal glasses. But there was an even bigger party in the sky, with millions and millions of stars.

For a while, Joana stood looking up, not thinking about anything. She was simply gazing in wonder at the vast joy of the night in the dark, luminous sky, with not a cloud or a shadow to be seen.

Then she went back into the house and closed the door.

'Will it be very long until supper?' she asked a maid she met in the corridor.

'It'll be a little while yet,' said the maid.

Then Joana went into the kitchen to see Gertrude the cook, who was a remarkable person, because she could touch hot things and not get burned and pick up the sharpest of knives without cutting herself, and she was in charge of everything and knew everything. Joana thought her the most important person she knew.

Gertrude had opened the oven to inspect the two Christmas turkeys. She was turning them and basting them with the cooking juices. The taut skin of the turkey breasts was already golden.

'May I ask you something, Gertrude?' said Joana.

Gertrude raised her head and her face looked as golden and roasted as the turkeys.

'What's that?' she asked.

'What presents do you think I'm going to get?'

'I don't know,' said Gertrude. 'I've no idea.'

Joana, however, had such confidence in Gertrude's knowledge of the world that she continued to ask questions.

'And do you think my friend will get many presents?'

'Which friend is that?'

'Manuel.'

'No, Manuel won't get any presents.'

'None at all?'

'No,' said Gertrude, shaking her head.

'But why?'

'Because he's poor, and poor people don't get presents.'

'But that's wrong, Gertrude.'

'Well, that's the way it is,' said Gertrude, closing the oven door.

Joana stood motionless in the middle of the kitchen. She accepted Gertrude's 'that's the way it is' because she knew that Gertrude understood how the world worked. Every morning, she would hear her haggling with the butcher, the fisherwoman and the woman selling fruit, and no one ever got the better of her.

She had been a cook for thirty years. And for thirty years she had been getting up at seven in the morning and working until eleven at night. And she knew everything that went on in the neighbourhood and everything that went on in other people's houses. And she knew all the gossip too. She knew all the recipes, she knew how to make all the cakes and knew all the different sorts of meat and fish and fruit and vegetables. She was never wrong. She knew everything there was to know about the world, and the things and the people in it.

However, what Gertrude had said grated on her as if it were a lie. Joana said nothing, though, and stood in the kitchen, thinking.

Suddenly, the door opened, and a maid appeared, saying: 'Your cousins have arrived.'

And Joana went to greet her cousins. A few minutes later, the grown-ups appeared too, and everyone went and sat round the table.

The Christmas Eve party had begun.

There was a smell of cinnamon and pinewood in the air. And everything on the table shone: the candles, the knives, the crystal glasses, the glass baubles, the golden pine cones. And the guests laughed and exchanged Happy Christmases. The glasses tinkled with the sound of happiness and parties. And Joana thought: 'Gertrude must be wrong. Christmas is a party for everyone. Tomorrow, Manuel will come and tell me all about his Christmas. He's sure to get presents too.'

And consoled by this thought, Joana felt almost as happy as she had before.

Christmas Eve supper was the same as it was every year. First, came the chicken soup, then the baked cod, then the roast turkey, then the crème caramel, then the eggy bread, and, finally, the pineapples. At the end, everyone stood up, the doors were flung wide, and they all went into the living room.

The lights were turned off, leaving only the candles on the tree.

Joana was nine years old, and although she had already seen the Christmas tree nine times, each time always felt as if it were the first.

The tree gave off a wonderful glow that touched everything with its light. It was as if a star had come down to Earth. It was Christmas. And that's why the tree was decorated with lights and its branches hung with exotic fruit, a reminder of the joy that had spread throughout the world on that other night many, many years ago.

And in the Christmas crib, the clay figures, the Child, the Virgin, St Joseph, the cow and the donkey, seemed to be continuing a quiet conversation that had never been interrupted - a conversation you could see but not hear.

Joana looked and looked and looked.

Sometimes her thoughts turned to her friend Manuel, then one of her cousins came and tugged at her sleeve and said: 'Joana, here are your presents.'

Joana opened the parcels and boxes one by one: a doll, a ball, books full of colourful drawings, a paintbox. Around her, everyone was laughing and chatting, showing each other the presents they'd received and all talking at the same time.

And Joana was thinking: 'Perhaps Manuel was given a toy car.'

And so the Christmas party went on.

The grown-ups sat on the chairs and sofas to talk, and the children sat on the floor to play.

Until someone said: 'It's half past eleven and almost time for midnight mass. And high time the children went to bed.'

Then people began to leave.

Joana's father and mother also left.

'Goodnight, my dear. Happy Christmas,' they said.

And the door shut.

A moment later, the maids left too.

The house became very silent. They had all gone to midnight mass, apart from old Gertrude, who was in the kitchen tidying up.

And so Joana went down to the kitchen. This

would be a good time to talk to Gertrude.

'Happy Christmas, Gertrude,' said Joana.

'Happy Christmas,' said Gertrude.

Joana fell silent then, before asking: 'Gertrude, is it true what you said before supper?'

'What did I say?'

'You said Manuel wouldn't get any Christmas presents because poor people don't get presents.'

'Of course it's true. I don't tell lies. He wouldn't have had presents or a Christmas tree or a stuffed turkey or any eggy bread. Poor people are poor and all they have is their poverty.'

'So what would his Christmas have been like?'

'Just like every other day.'

'And what is every other day like?'

'A bowl of soup and a bit of bread.'

'Is that true, Gertrude?'

'Of course it's true. But you'd better go to bed now, because it's nearly midnight.'

'Goodnight,' said Joana, and left the kitchen.

She went up the stairs to her bedroom. Her presents lay on her bed. She looked at them one by one. And she was thinking: 'A doll, a ball, a paintbox and books. Those are exactly the presents I wanted. I was given everything I wanted, but no one gave Manuel anything.'

And sitting on the edge of the bed with her presents, Joana started imagining what coldness and darkness and poverty would be like. She started imagining what Christmas Eve would be like in that house that wasn't really a house, but a hut, a stable.

'It must be so cold!' she thought.

'It must be so dark!' she thought.

'It must be so sad!' she thought.

And she began imagining the dark, freezing cold stable where Manuel would be sleeping on the straw, warmed only by the breath of a cow and a donkey.

'Tomorrow, I'm going to give him my presents,' she said.

Then she sighed and thought: 'No, tomorrow it won't be the same. Christmas Eve is when you should get your presents, and it's Christmas Eve now.'

She went over to the window, opened the shutters and peered out at the street. No one was passing. Manuel would be sleeping. He would only come to see her the next morning. In the distance, she could see a large, dark shadow: the pine forest.

Then, coming from the church tower, loud and clear, she heard the twelve strokes of midnight.

'Now,' thought Joana. 'I have to go now. I have to go there now, tonight, so that he'll have some presents on Christmas Eve.'

She went over to her wardrobe, took out a coat and put it on. Then she picked up the ball, the paintbox and the books. She considered taking him the doll as well, but thought better of it. After all, he was a boy and wouldn't be interested in dolls.

Joana tiptoed down the stairs, and every stair creaked, but Gertrude was making so much clatter in the kitchen putting things away that she heard nothing.

A door in the dining room gave directly onto the garden. Joana opened it and went out, leaving it on the latch.

Then she crossed the garden. Alex and Chiribita both barked.

'It's me,' Joana said.

And when they heard her voice, the two dogs stopped barking.

Then she opened the garden gate and went out.

The Star

When she found herself alone in the street, she was tempted to turn back. The trees seemed gigantic, and their bare branches filled the sky with shapes like fantastical birds. And the street seemed to be alive, even though it was completely deserted. At that hour, no one was passing. Everyone was at midnight mass. Safe inside their gardens, the houses had all their doors and windows closed. There wasn't a soul to be seen, only things, but Joana had the feeling that the things were looking at her and listening to her as if they were people.

'I'm afraid,' she thought, but resolved to keep walking straight ahead and not look at anything.

When she reached the end of the road, she turned down an alleyway between two walls. At the end of that alleyway, she saw flat, empty fields. There, without walls or trees or houses, she could see the night more clearly, the lofty, brilliant dome of the night sky. The silence was so loud it seemed to be singing. Far off in the distance, she could see the dark mass of the pine trees.

'Will I ever get there?' thought Joana, but kept walking.

Her feet sank into the icy grass. Out in the open, a sharp snowy wind cut her face like a knife.

'I'm cold,' thought Joana, but kept walking.

As she came closer, the pine forest grew and grew until it was vast.

Joana stopped for a moment in the middle of the fields.

'I wonder where the hut is?' she thought.

And she looked all around her for a path to follow.

But there was no path to her right, no path to her left and no path straight ahead.

'How am I going to find the way?' she thought.

Then she looked up, and saw a star moving very slowly across the sky.

'That star looks like a friend,' she thought.

And she began to follow the star.

Until, that is, she entered the forest. Then, in an instant, the shadows closed about her, huge shadows, green and purple and black and blue, were dancing around her, waving their arms. And the breeze blowing through the needles of the pine trees seemed to be murmuring incomprehensible words. Finding herself surrounded by voices and shadows, Joana felt afraid and wanted to run away, but, looking up, she saw that, high in the sky, beyond all the shadows, the star continued to move. And so she followed the star.

She was already deep in the forest when she seemed to hear footsteps.

'Could it be a wolf?' she thought.

She stopped to listen. The sound of footsteps came closer, until she saw, emerging from the trees, a very tall figure coming towards her.

'Could it be a thief?' she thought.

But the figure stopped right in front of her, and she saw that the 'figure' was, in fact, a king. He had a gold crown on his head and around his shoulders a long blue cloak embroidered with diamonds.

'Good evening,' said Joana.

'Good evening,' said the king. 'What's your name?'

'Joana,' she said.

'And my name is Melchior,' said the king.

Then he asked: 'Where are you going all alone and at this late hour?'

'I'm following that star,' she said.

'So am I,' said the king, 'I'm following that star too.'

And together they continued through the forest.

Again Joana heard footsteps. And another figure emerged out of the shadows of the night.

This figure wore a crown studded with diamonds and, around his shoulders, a red mantle sewn with emeralds and sapphires.

'Good evening,' she said. 'My name's Joana and I'm following the star.'

'I'm following the star too,' said the king, 'and my name is Gaspar.'

And they continued together through the forest.

Again Joana heard the sound of footsteps, and a third figure emerged out of the blue shadows and the dark pine trees.

He was wearing a white turban and around his shoulders a long green mantle embroidered with pearls. His face was black.

'Good evening,' she said. 'My name is Joana, and we're all following the star.'

'I'm following the star too,' said the king, 'and my name is Balthasar.'

And together the four of them continued through the night forest.

Dry twigs snapped beneath their feet, the breeze murmured in the branches, and the great embroidered cloaks of the three kings from the Orient glittered among the green, purple and blue shadows.

When they were almost at the edge of the forest, they saw a light in the distance, and above that light the star stopped.

And they continued to walk until they reached the place where the star had stopped, and there Joana saw a hut with no door, but she saw no darkness or shadows or sadness, for the hut was filled with light, with the glow from the Angels.

And then Joana saw her friend Manuel. He was lying on the straw between the cow and the donkey and was fast asleep, a smile on his face.

Around him, kneeling mid-air, were the Angels. His body seemed weightless and made of a light that cast no shadows.

The Angels had their hands clasped in prayer. This then was Manuel's Christmas, lit by the light of the Angels.

'Oh,' said Joana, 'it's just like the Nativity scene!'

'Yes,' said King Balthasar, 'it's exactly like the Nativity.'

Then Joana knelt down and placed her presents on the ground.

The Danish Knight

Denmark lies in the North of Europe. The winters there are long and harsh, and the nights are long too, while the days are short and grey and icy cold. The snow covers the land and the rooftops, the rivers freeze over, the birds fly south in search of sun, and the trees lose their leaves. In the midst of those bare, frozen forests only the pine trees remain green. With their branches covered in fine, hard, shiny needles, they seem to be the only things alive in the midst of that great, still, white silence.

Many years ago, tens and hundreds of years ago, in a certain place in Denmark, in the far north of the country, near the sea, there was a large forest of lime trees, pines, firs and oaks. A Knight lived in that forest with his family, in a house built in a clearing surrounded by birches. Opposite their front door stood a pine tree, the tallest tree in the forest.

In spring, the birches were covered in light, fresh, young leaves, which trembled in the slightest breeze. Then the snow would disappear and the thaw would release the waters of the nearby river, which began to sing again, night and day, among the grasses, the moss and the pebbles. Then the forest would fill up with mushrooms and wild strawberries. The birds would return from the south, the ground become covered in flowers, and the squirrels could once more be seen leaping from tree to tree. The air was peopled with voices and bees, and the breeze whispered in the branches.

On green and golden summer mornings, the children would set off very early, a wicker basket over their left arm, to pick flowers, strawberries, blackberries or mushrooms. They would weave garlands to wear on their head or else float them down the river. And they would sing and dance on the fine grass beneath the luminous, tremulous shade of the oaks and the lime trees. Once summer was over, the October wind would strip the trees bare of their leaves, and then winter would return, and the forest would again become still and silent, imprisoned in its vestments of snow and ice.

And yet the biggest festival of the year, the greatest source of joy, happened in the winter, right in the middle of winter, on the long, cold night of Christmas Eve.

Then the Knight's house would be filled with a great hustle and bustle. The family would all get together along with friends, relatives, servants and workers from the forest. And for many days before, the cook would be busy baking honey cakes, the servants would be sweeping the corridors and the stairs, and washing, waxing and polishing everything else. Great wreaths of holly were hung above all the doors, and everything was spick and span. The excited children would scamper from room to room, race up and down the stairs, run errands, help with the preparations. Or they would sit, silently daydreaming, looking out of the windows at the vast forest and thinking about the marvellous stories of how those three kings from the East travelled to the nativity in Bethlehem.

Outside, all was ice, wind and snow, but inside, all was warmth and light, laughter and joy.

And on Christmas Eve, in front of the huge fireplace, a very long table would be laid, and the Knight, his wife, their children, their relatives and their servants would all take their places.

The kitchen boys would bring in great joints of roast meat and everyone would eat and laugh, and drink mulled wine and honey ale.

Once supper was over, the storytelling would begin. One person would tell stories about wolves and bears, another stories about gnomes and dwarves. A woman would recount the legend of Tristan and Isolde, and an old man with a white beard would recount the legend of Alfred, King of Denmark, and of Sigurd, but the loveliest stories were always the Christmas stories about the Three Kings, the shepherds and the Angels.

Christmas Eve was the same every year. Always the same party, always the same supper, always the big holly wreaths above the doors, always the same stories. And yet, those customs so often repeated, those stories so often heard, seemed more beautiful and more mysterious with each year that passed.

Until one Christmas, something totally unexpected happened in that household. When supper was over, the Knight turned to his family, to his friends and to his servants, and said: 'We have always celebrated and commemorated Christmas Eve together. And it has always been an occasion full of peace and joy. In a year's time, though, I won't be here.'

'Why not?' asked everyone, astonished.

'I'm going away,' he said. 'I'm going on a pilgrimage to the Holy Land, and I want to spend next Christmas in the grotto where Christ was born and where the shepherds, the Three Kings and the Angels all prayed. I want to pray there too. I will leave in the spring, and this time next year, I will be in Bethlehem. After Christmas, though, I will come back, and in two years' time, God willing, we will all be reunited again.'

In those days, journeys were long, dangerous and difficult, and to travel from Denmark to Palestine was a big adventure. It would be far from easy for anyone making the journey to send back news, and often they might not return at all. This is why the Knight's wife was so upset and anxious at this news. Yet she didn't try to persuade her husband to stay, because no one should stop a pilgrim from going on a pilgrimage.

The next spring, the Knight left his forest and headed for the nearest town, which was a sea port. There he boarded a ship, and, borne along by a good northerly wind, he arrived on the Palestinian coast well before Christmas. From there he joined other pilgrims travelling to Jerusalem.

He visited the holy places one by one. He prayed on Golgotha and in Gethsemane, washed his face in the waters of the Jordan and, in the luminous Galilee winter, saw the blue waters of the Sea of Galilee. In the streets of Jerusalem, in the silent testimony of the stones, he sought the trail of blood and suffering left there by the Son of Man as he was persecuted, humiliated and condemned. He walked into the hills of Judea, which had once heard Jesus pronounce the new commandment of love.

When Christmas Eve arrived, the Knight visited the grotto in Bethlehem, and there he spent all night praying. He prayed in the very place where the Virgin, St Joseph, the ox, the ass, the shepherds, the Three Kings and the Angels had worshipped the newborn babe. And when the church bells struck twelve at midnight, he thought he heard the Angels' prayer in a song sung by countless multitudes: 'Glory to God in the highest and on earth peace to all men and women of good will.'

Then he felt descend upon him a great peace and a great sense of trust, and, weeping with joy, he kissed the stones of the grotto.

That night, the Knight prayed for a long time. He prayed for an end to poverty and to war, he prayed for peace and joy in the world. He asked

God to make him a man of good will, a man with a clear, direct will, capable of loving others. And he also asked the Angels to protect and guide him on his return journey, so that, in a year's time, he would be able to celebrate Christmas at home surrounded by his family.

After Christmas, the Knight spent another two months in Palestine, visiting the places that had seen Abraham and David, the Ark of the Covenant, the Queen of Sheba and her caravan of camels laden with perfumes, the Babylonian armies, the Roman legions, and Christ preaching to the multitudes.

Then, towards the end of February, he bade farewell to Jerusalem and, along with other pilgrims, set off for the port of Jaffa.

Among those pilgrims was a merchant from Venice, with whom the Knight struck up a great friendship.

In Jaffa, they were obliged to wait for good weather and could only board ship in mid-March.

Once at sea, they were caught in a storm. The ship would rise up on the crest of a wave only to come crashing down again, shuddering from end to end. The masts and the cables creaked and groaned. The waves beat furiously against the hull of the ship and swept over the stern. The ship rolled now to the left, now to the right, and the sailors pumped frantically so that she did not fill up with water. The wind ripped the sails to shreds and left ship and passengers adrift and at the mercy of the sea.

'Ah,' thought the Knight. 'I will never see my homeland again.'

After five days, though, the wind eased, the sky cleared, and the sea smoothed its waters. The sailors hoisted new sails, and with a favourable breeze, they were able to reach the port of Ravenna on the Adriatic coast, in the land of Italy.

The ship, however, was too badly battered to continue the voyage.

'I'll wait for another ship,' said the Knight.

He was astonished at the beauty of Ravenna. He never wearied of admiring the beautiful churches, the lofty naves, the elegant arches, the rows of slender columns. More than anything, though, he admired the multicoloured mosaics showing the tall figures of queens and saints gazing down on him with their large eyes.

'Listen,' said the Merchant to the Knight. 'Don't wait here for another ship. Come with me to Venice. If you find Ravenna astonishing, you will find my city built on water even more so. From Venice you can continue overland to the port of Genoa. That way, you will travel across the north of Italy and visit its beautiful, wealthy cities famed throughout Europe. Ships leave Genoa for Flanders all the time. And from Flanders, it will take no time at all to reach your homeland.'

The Knight took the Merchant's advice and travelled on to Venice with him.

Built on the shores of the Adriatic Sea on small islands and wooden piles, Venice was, at the time, one of the most powerful cities in the world. The Knight found everything he saw there a source of astonishment. The streets were canals travelled by slender, dark, narrow boats. The palaces grew out of the water, which reflected the marble, the stuccoed walls and the columns.

In vast St Mark's Square, opposite the equally vast cathedral and the tall, tall belltower, the Knight could scarcely believe what his eyes were seeing.

The light, airy city rested on the green waters, accompanied by its own image.

The men he passed were dressed in damask and women wore dresses with embroidered hems that trailed on the ground. The sound of voices, laughter, songs and bells filled the evening air.

The Knight had never imagined such wealth and beauty could exist in the world. He never tired of looking at the marble steps, the gold mosaics, the solemn bronze statues, the shimmering waters of the canals reflecting the delicate columns of pink palaces, the bridges, the sumptuously stuccoed walls, the churches and the towers. The city seemed to him fantastical, unreal, born of the sea, and composed of mirages and reflections. It was just like one of those enchanted cities that fairies summon up from the depths of lakes and mirrors.

The Merchant invited the Knight to stay in his palace, and, in his honour, organised many parties and other amusements. During the day, they travelled the city by gondola. They visited churches decorated with mosaics and paintings, and stopped at market stalls selling rare birds, lace, Oriental fabrics, pearl necklaces, sapphire rings, gold and silver spurs, enamels and ornate coffers, swords and daggers with turquoise-and-ivory-incrusted hilts, goblets and bottles made of the finest glass, and as many-coloured as the waters and as light as foam.

At night, to the sound of the lute, they dined in the great hall of blue and green marble. On the table, the servants placed huge platters of roast pheasant, bowls overflowing with fruit, and served red wine in transparent glasses.

Outside, beneath the blue light of the moon, Venice appeared to hang in the air.

One night, after supper, the Venetian and the Dane sat talking on the balcony. On the other side of the canal they could see a beautiful palace with slender, carved columns.

'Who lives there?' asked the Knight.

'Jacopo Orso lives there alone with his servants, but Vanina also lived there once. She was deemed to be the most beautiful girl in Venice. She had lost both her parents, and Orso was her guardian. When she was still a child, her guardian promised her in marriage to a relative of his called Arrigo. When Vanina turned eighteen, however, she didn't want to marry Arrigo because she thought him old, ugly and boring. Then Orso shut her up in the house and would only let her go outside in his company and then only on Sundays, to attend mass. For all the other days of the week, Vanina remained a prisoner in the palace, sighing over her embroidery, and watched and spied upon by her maids. At night, though, when Orso and the maids were sleeping, Vanina would open her bedroom window, lean on the balcony and comb her hair. Her lustrous blonde hair was so long that it hung down over the balcony and was reflected in the water. And so perfumed was her hair that, even from far away, you could smell its perfume on the breeze. And the young men in Venice would come at night to watch Vanina combing her hair, but none dared approach her, because her guardian had let it be known throughout the city that anyone foolish enough to court her would be stabbed to death by one of his thugs.

And so young, beautiful, loveless Vanina would sit in the palace and sigh.

One day, though, a man arrived in Venice who was not afraid of Jacopo Orso. His name was Guidobaldo, and he was the captain of a ship. His dark hair was blue-black like the wing of a crow, and his skin was burned by the sun and the salt air. A handsomer sailor had never been seen on the Rialto.

One night, Guidobaldo was travelling the canal by gondola, when he smelled that marvellous perfume. He looked up and saw Vanina combing her hair.

He steered his gondola closer to the balcony and said: 'Such lovely, perfumed hair deserves a golden comb.'

Vanina smiled and threw him the ivory comb she was using.

The following night, at the same hour, the young captain again came by in his gondola.

Vanina shook out her hair and said: 'I can't comb my hair tonight because I have no comb.'

'But you do, for I have brought you one made of gold, although even gold doesn't shine as brightly as your hair.'

Then Vanina attached a ribbon to a basket and lowered it down to the water, so that Guidobaldo could place his gift in it.

From that night on, the most beautiful girl in Venice had a suitor.

When the news spread, the captain's friends warned Guidobaldo that he was risking his life, because Orso would never forgive him. But Guidobaldo was strong and fearless, and merely shrugged and laughed.

A month later, he went to knock at her guardian's door.

'What do you want?' asked the old man.

'I want Vanina's hand in marriage.'

'Vanina is engaged to Arrigo and will never marry anyone else. Leave Venice now. I give you one day, and if you have not left by sunset tomorrow, I will send seven men with seven daggers to kill you.'

Guidobaldo listened, smiled, bowed and left.

That night, in the silence of the night, his gondola stopped beneath the balcony. A basket attached to a ribbon was again thrown down, and this time the young captain placed in it a silken ladder.

The basket was hauled back up, and the ladder, once unrolled, was tied to the pink marble balcony. Then Vanina climbed lightly, nimbly down the ladder, her hair lifted by the breeze.

Guidobaldo wrapped her in his dark cape, and the gondola slipped away down the canal and disappeared into the October mist.

The following morning, the maids found Vanina gone and ran to alert her guardian.

Jacopo Orso summoned Arrigo and, along with Orso's thugs, they set off for the quay.

When they arrived, Guidobaldo's ship had vanished.

'Tell me everything you know,' said Orso to an old sailor who was an acquaintance of his.

And the man said: 'The captain and your ward arrived here at midnight. They sent for a priest, who married them in the small chapel known as the sailors' chapel. As soon as the ceremony was over, they boarded the ship, and, at the first light of day, their ship weighed anchor, the sails were hoisted and off they went.'

Jacopo Orso gazed off into the distance. There was no sign of the ship, because the breeze was blowing from the land. The gently rippling waters were green and clear and flecked with silver.

The guardian and Arrigo went to put their case to the Signoria of Venice and to the Doge. Then they despatched four ships to pursue the fugitives: one sailed North, the second East, the third South and the fourth sailed West. But the sea is a very large place and there are many ports, many bays, many maritime cities, many islands. And Vanina and Guidobaldo were never seen again.

When he had finished his story, the merchant filled two glasses with wine, and he and the Danish knight drank to the health of Vanina and the captain.

And thus a whole month passed in conversations, parties, suppers and walks about the city. At the end of that month, the Merchant said to the Knight: 'Don't leave. Stay here with me. Become my business partner and make your life here. There's no better place in the world than Venice. Every day here is full of joys and surprises. Stay with me.'

'No,' said the Knight. 'I have to leave. I promised my wife, my children, my relatives and servants that I would be with them next Christmas Eve. I will leave in three days' time.'

And three days later, mounted on a fine horse given to him by the Merchant, the Knight left Venice.

As well as the gift of the horse, his friend also gave him letters of introduction to the most powerful men in the cities of Northern Italy, which meant he would be well received everywhere.

April filled the land with flowers. Every stream was singing, the sky was blue, the air warm, the breeze light. And the Knight rode on over plains, valleys, hills and mountains.

On the Merchant's advice, the Knight had decided that, halfway to Genoa, he would make a detour south in order to visit the celebrated city of Florence.

He passed through Ferrara and Bologna and saw the towers of San Gimignano. He slept in inns or sought shelter in monasteries.

And at the beginning of May, he arrived in Florence.

Seen from the verdant hills above the city, its red rooftops, towers, belfries and cupolas stood out against the blue sky. The Knight crossed the old bridge over the river, a bridge flanked by small shops selling leather goods, coral necklaces, swords and knives, plates of pewter and silver, wools, silks, and gold jewellery.

Then he walked along streets lined with palaces, across broad squares and past black and white marble churches with huge ornate bronze doors. Everywhere he saw statues, statues made of pale marble and statues made of bronze, and still others made of painted terracotta. And the Knight was as astonished by the beauty of Florence as he had been by the beauty of Venice. Here, though, everything seemed somehow graver and more austere.

He went in search of the house of the banker Averardo, for whom his Venetian friend had given him a letter of introduction.

The banker welcomed him gladly and made him a guest in his house.

It was a beautiful house, although less luxurious than those Venetian palaces. It had a library full of ancient manuscripts, and the walls were hung with marvellous paintings.

In the evening, the banker's friends arrived.

They all sat down to supper and, while they ate and drank, they talked. And the Knight's astonishment only grew.

In his country, he would seek out the company of troubadors and travellers to tell him of their adventures and legendary tales from the past, whereas in that house in Florence, those men were discussing the movements of the sun and of light, and the mysteries of heaven and earth. They spoke of mathematics, astronomy, philosophy. They spoke of ancient statues and paintings on which the paint was barely dry. They spoke of the past, the present and the future. And they spoke of poetry, music and architecture. It seemed as if all Earthly knowledge was gathered there in that room.

Halfway through supper, a discussion arose about the work of Giotto.

'Who's Giotto?' asked the Knight.

A man sitting on the opposite side of the table, a handsome man with long curly hair, said: 'Giotto was a painter from the last century, a student of Cimabue's.'

'And who was Cimabue?' asked the Knight.

The man, whose name was Filippo, smiled and answered: 'Just as Adam was the first man on Earth, so Cimabue was the first painter in Italy. And he was the one who discovered the talent of the young Giotto. This happened one spring morning over a hundred years ago. Cimabue was returning from a journey and, when he was almost halfway home, he saw on the side of a hill, in a wild and solitary spot, a great rock covered in drawings. They were simple drawings, but full of truth and beauty.

"Who could have made these drawings?" exclaimed Cimabue, amazed and surprised.

And leaving the path, he tethered his horse to a tree and decided to examine other rocks that he could see in the distance.

After walking for nearly half an hour among pine trees, cypresses, heather and gorse, he found a flock of sheep and their shepherd.

While the sheep grazed on the tender April grass, the shepherd was kneeling before a rock face, drawing. He was a boy of about twelve, and so intent, so absorbed was he in his work, that he didn't even notice Cimabue approach or hear his footsteps. He was drawing a lamb. And there was such love, truth and beauty in the drawing that Cimabue's heart was filled with joy and wonder.

"Listen, my boy," he said, "who taught you to draw?"

Hearing this voice and seeing this man from the city, the boy leapt to his feet. Then he smiled and answered: "No one taught me. I learned by myself."

"Where do you live?"

"Here in the hills."

"What do you do?"

"I keep my sheep."

"What's your name"

"Giotto."

"Well, Giotto, leave your sheep and come with me to Florence. You will be my student and one day you will be a great painter."

And so it was. The shepherd went with Cimabue, who taught him all the secrets of his art. Every day, the student astonished his teacher with his talent, and soon he astonished all of Florence. Giotto thus became the most famous painter of his day. And Dante, whom he painted and who became his friend, spoke of him in his poem.'

'Who was Dante?' asked the Knight.

'Dante was Italy's greatest poet, one who knew the secrets of this world and the next, for he saw, when alive, what we will only see when dead.'

'How did he do that?' asked the Knight.

'It's such an extraordinary story that many people believe Dante dreamed it.'

'Do, please, tell me that story,' said the Knight.

And Filippo began: 'When Dante was nine years old, he saw a young girl in the street, the same age as him. Her name was Beatrice. Beatrice was the most beautiful child in all Florence: her bright eyes were green, her neck long and slender, her hair like spun gold that fluttered in the breeze. And she walked along with a pure, grave, honest air reminiscent of the Madonnas painted in our churches. Dante loved her from that very first moment, from that very first encounter. A few years later, when she was still extremely young, Beatrice died. Her death was a torment to Dante, and, in order to forget his grief, he began to lead a life of folly and sin. Until on Good Friday, 8th April 1300, he found himself in a dark forest and there appeared before him a panther, a lion and a she-wolf. Dante looked around him and saw what looked like a shadow passing by. He called out for help, and the shadow said: "I am the shade of Virgil, the poet who died more than a thousand years ago, and I come at Beatrice's request to guide you to the place where she awaits you."

Dante followed Virgil. First, they passed through the gates of Hell, over which are written the words: "Abandon all hope, ye who enter here."

Then they journeyed through the nine circles of Hell inhabited by the souls of the damned. They saw people pelted by a constant rain of mud, or eternally buffeted by contrary winds, or condemned to live forever in the fiery flames, and they saw traitors permanently imprisoned in lakes of ice. Everywhere there were monsters and demons, and Dante, trembling with fear, clung to Virgil. Everywhere it was as dark as a coal mine, for this was the subterranean kingdom, with no sun, no moon and no stars, lit only by the flames of Hell.

Having travelled through every one of Hell's circles, they returned to the light of the sun and reached Purgatory, which is a mountain in the middle of an island that reaches up as far as the sky. There Dante and Virgil saw the souls who, through acts of penitence and prayers, are on their way to Paradise. There were no demons to be seen, instead, Angels bright as stars would appear on each new path.

Finally, they reached the Earthly Paradise, which is on top of the mountain of Purgatory. Among lawns and woods, fountains and flowers, Dante again met Beatrice. On her head she wore a white veil, wreathed about with olive leaves, and over her shoulders a green cloak, and her dress was flame-red. She was in a carriage drawn by a strange beast, half-lion and half-bird.

"Dante," she said, "I summoned you here to cure you of all your sins. You have seen how the souls in Hell suffer, and you've seen the terrible acts of penance done by those in Purgatory. Now I will take you with me up into Paradise, so that you can see the happiness and joy of the good and the just."

Guided by Beatrice, the poet travelled the nine

circles of Paradise. They walked among stars and planets surrounded by Angels and singing. And there they saw the souls of the just filled with glory and joy. When they reached the tenth sphere, Beatrice bade farewell to her friend and said: "Go back to Earth and set down in a book all the things you have seen. That way you will teach men to hate evil and to desire good."

Dante returned to this world and carried out Beatrice's wishes. He wrote a long, remarkable poem called *The Divine Comedy*, in which he told of his journey through the kingdom of the dead.

News of this journey caused great amazement in Florence. When Dante walked down the street, everyone would turn to look at him, for, they said, his beard was "still singed by the flames of the Inferno through which he had walked".'

'That truly is the most extraordinary story I've ever heard,' said the Knight. 'I can understand why Dante should have been received with such amazement and curiosity. And I imagine that, from then on, he must have been seen as a man of great authority, and was respected and listened to by all his fellow citizens.'

'He should have been,' said Filippo, 'but he wasn't. Having travelled through the three realms of death, the poet returned to Florence to find a city embroiled in political struggles. At the time, there were two parties dividing Italy: the Guelphs and the Ghibellines. Dante was a Ghibelline, and in that year of 1300 he was elected to the city council. Some time later, though, his party was defeated, and he was sent into exile. Subsequently, his enemies condemned him to be burned alive. Fortunately, he was far from Florence by then, and thus escaped death and torture. He could never return to his birthplace, though, and so lived out the rest of his life like a political refugee wandering from city to city. It was during that exile, separated from Beatrice by death and from Florence by the injustice of other men, that Dante wrote *The Divine Comedy.*'

When Filippo stopped speaking, a silence fell.

Then two wise men began discussing the laws that govern the seven planets. And the Knight marvelled at everything he heard and decided to stay longer in that city.

By day, he walked the streets and squares and visited the monasteries, palaces, libraries and churches. At night, he listened to the learned conversations of Averardo's friends.

A month later, the banker said to him: 'Why don't you become my business partner and make your life here in Florence. There may be wealthier, more powerful cities in the world, but none more learned. If you want to study Mathematics and Geometry, stay in Florence. If you want to study the golden mean, stay in Florence. If you want to know how the planets move in the sky, stay in Florence. If you want to understand sculpture, painting, architecture and poetry, then stay in Florence.'

The Knight smiled and answered: 'Thank you for your kind invitation. Since being here, I have marvelled every day at everything I see, hear and learn. But far away, in my country in the North, my children, my wife and my servants are waiting for me. I want to spend next Christmas Eve with them as I promised. In three days' time I must leave.'

Then Averardo gave him a letter of introduction to a rich trader in Flanders, a customer and friend of his.

Three days later, the Knight left Florence.

He was in a hurry now to reach the port of Genoa and embark on one of the ships which, in early summer, sail from Italy to Bruges, Ghent and Antwerp.

However, towards the end of his journey, when he was only a short distance from Genoa, he fell ill. This was due perhaps to the scorching sun that beat down on him as he rode through valleys and over mountains, or the water he drank from a well where the green lizards went to drink at night.

Shaking with fever, he knocked on the door of a monastery. The monks who took him in had a hard time saving him, because the Knight's blood appeared to be infected and he was delirious for whole days and nights. In his delirium he imagined that he would never again reach his own country because Venice kept rising up from the waters and dragging him down with it into the depths of the sea, or because the statues of Florence formed bronze and marble armies that refused to let him pass.

The monks gave him herbal teas made from the roots of flowers, pills made from aloes, potions made from honey and mulled wine, as well as mysterious powders and poultices made from flour and herbs. Gradually the fever subsided, but it took a whole month and a half to cease completely. The Knight wanted to continue his journey then, but he was so weak and thin and pale that the monks would not allow him to leave.

He had to wait for more than a month in that small, tranquil, silent monastery. Lying in his whitewashed cell, he would listen to the murmuring fountains in the courtyard and to the singing of the monks. Then in the evening, he would stroll around the cloisters, admiring the pale frescoes depicting miracles performed by the saints. On the right-hand wall, St Anthony could be seen preaching to the fishes, and on the left-hand side St Francis was making a pact with the wolf of Gubbio.

In the middle of the cloister stood a fountain, around which grew carnations and white roses, and the blue sky above was criss-crossed by swallows.

A great sense of peace emanated from the cloisters, from the murmuring fountain, from the flowers, the frescoes and the birds, as if men, animals, plants and stones had together founded a kingdom based on co-operation and love.

In this peaceful world, the Knight grew stronger by the day, until, after five weeks of rest, he could finally say goodbye to the monks and continue his journey to Genoa.

However, by the time he reached that great sea port, it was already late September, and all the ships bound for Flanders had left. He walked up and down the quay, spoke to ship's captains and to the ship's owners, but the answer they gave him was always the same: he would have to wait several months before he would find a ship willing to take him to Flanders. At first, the Knight was in despair at this news and for two days, he neither ate nor slept. Then, however, he recovered his good spirits and decided to travel on horseback to Bruges.

He crossed the Alps, and crossed the fields, plains, valleys and mountains of France.

Now he stopped only to eat and sleep, eager to reach home before Christmas.

When he arrived in Flanders, however, it was already winter, and the first snow was falling on rooftops and fields.

The Knight travelled to Antwerp then, and there sought out the Flemish trader for whom the banker Averardo had given him a letter of introduction.

He found the trader at home, warming his hands by the fire. He was wearing a beautiful long green robe edged with black fur. He welcomed the traveller and invited him to stay in his house.

At supper, the Knight was astonished by the food he was served, for it was seasoned with spices entirely unknown to him.

The trader shook his head, laughed and said: 'You obviously know little of the New World.'

Rather indignant at this statement, the Knight began to tell him about his journey so far, and when he finished, the trader said: 'You tell a fine story, but very soon another guest will arrive who will tell you some even more amazing stories.'

Indeed, shortly afterwards, someone knocked at the door of the house, footsteps were heard on the stairs, and a tall, burly man came into the room; he looked slightly dishevelled, had sunburnt skin and a rolling gait.

'This is the captain of one of my ships,' said the trader. 'He returned from a voyage just two days ago.'

The new arrival set down three small chests on the table and said: 'Here are three samples of the merchandise I've brought back.'

The first chest was full of small pearls, the second was full of gold, and the third was full of pepper.

The Knight was amazed at what he saw, for in those days, pepper was almost as rare as gold.

The owner of the house put more wood on the fire, poured wine for his guests, and then they sat down together by the hearth.

At the request of the trader, the captain began to talk about his voyages. He described how he had been a sailor since he was a boy, and had travelled to all the ports of Europe from the Baltic Sea to the Mediterranean. However, he had mainly only travelled between Flanders and the Iberian Peninsula, and, one day, he felt an urge to go further, to visit unknown lands. He decided to join one of the Portuguese expeditions heading south in search of new countries, and duly set off for Lisbon, where he embarked on a caravel that was leaving to explore the coast of Africa.

They sailed from the River Tejo to the Canary Islands, where they stopped for a few days. Then they continued on towards Africa, round Cape Bojador and onwards, within sight of deserts seared by the sun, with no trees and no men. They anchored alongside the peninsular of Ras Nouadhibou, sheltered by high cliffs. There, some dark-skinned men, wrapped in flowing cloaks and mounted on camels, came to the shore to negotiate with the Portuguese. Then the caravels continued on south, still further south. A constant breeze filled the great sails, and the masts and ropes creaked gently, until, beyond the endless bare, empty coasts, bereft of trees and shade, the first palm trees appeared. These were followed by thick, green forests that covered everything from the white beaches to the distant blue mountains. And out of those forests came naked black men, who boarded rafts and approached the ships. The Portuguese sailors were under orders to speak to them, but this proved difficult. The rafts did not usually come very close to the ship, or else the black men would vanish into the trees as soon as the caravels dropped anchor, and from the safety of the forest would shoot poisoned arrows at any sailors who disembarked.

However, the caravel also called in at places where the Africans and the Portuguese already knew each other and had already done business together. And sometimes, in places where no ship had ever stopped, they would be welcomed with great excitement and celebration. The black men would come to meet the sailors, singing and dancing, and the sailors would respond to that warm welcome by dancing and singing in the manner of their own country.

Often, though, communication between both parties advanced no further, since neither understood each other's language, and even the Berber interpreters were unfamiliar with the languages spoken in such far-flung places. This linguistic gulf was the cause of many deaths and many battles. One day, for example, a caravel anchored off a large beautiful bay surrounded by lush forests. On the long beach of white sand, a small group of Africans were watching the ship. The captain decided to send two small skiffs to try and establish contact with them. However, as soon as the skiffs touched land, the Africans fled into the trees.

'Perhaps they were afraid when they saw that we are many and they are few,' said a Portuguese man called Pero Dias.

So he asked his companions to leave him there in one of the skiffs, while they moved farther off. His companions thought this plan too dangerous and at first refused. Pero Dias, however, was so insistent that they ended up doing as he asked and they rowed some distance from the shore.

As soon as he was alone, Pero Dias positioned himself in the middle of the beach, where he laid out the brightly coloured fabrics the sailors had brought as gifts. Then he withdrew to the sea's edge, leaned on the side of the skiff and waited. After some time had passed, a man emerged from the trees; he was carrying a long, slender spear in one hand, and he approached, black and naked against the white sand. He advanced slowly, step by step, watching for any move the white man standing by the skiff might make. When he reached the fabrics laid out on the sand, he examined them with great delight. Then he looked up at Pero Dias and smiled. Pero Dias smiled back and took a few steps forwards. There was a brief pause. Then, by mutual agreement, the two men, still smiling, walked towards each other. When they were only about six paces from each other, they stopped.

'I come in peace,' said Dias in his own language.

The African smiled and responded with a few words that Dias had never heard before.

'I come in peace,' said Dias in Arabic this time.

The African smiled again and again repeated those words Dias could not understand.

'I come in peace,' said Dias in Berber.

Again the African smiled and again he responded with those same strange words.

Then Pero Dias began to speak using gestures. He made the gesture of drinking, and the African pointed to the forest. He made the gesture of eating, and the African once again pointed to the forest. Dias then beckoned to him to get into the skiff.

At this, the African shook his head and took a step back. Seeing him retreat and hoping to establish trust, Dias began to sing and dance. The African followed his example, leaping and singing and laughing. For some time they continued to dance for each other. However, Pero Dias became so carried away with his dancing and his mimicry that he suddenly drew his sword, which glittered in the sun. That glittering blade so startled the African that he jumped back, trembling. Pero Dias made a reassuring gesture, but the African began to run away. Dias ran after him and grabbed him by the arm. Feeling trapped, the African began to struggle, first out of fear, then out of anger. He responded to Dias' supposedly soothing words and gestures with hoarse cries and guttural sounds. Pero Dias' companions saw the struggle and began to row towards the shore.

When he saw this, the African thought he was lost, and wielded his spear. Pero Dias tried to parry the blow with his sword and both fell to the ground, each impaled on the other's weapon.

The Portuguese sailors jumped out of their skiff and ran over to the two prone bodies. From the breasts of both men, black and white, flowed two streams of blood.

'Look,' said a boy, 'their blood is exactly the same colour.'

The captain came then, with more of the crew, and for an hour, they mourned the outcome of that sad encounter.

The sun was rising in the sky and the midday heat was not far off. Not knowing when they might next disembark, the captain resolved not to take

Pero Dias' dead body on board. Instead, the two bodies were buried right there, on the beach. And with the spear of the pagan and the sword of the Christian, the sailors made a cross, which they stuck in the sand between the graves of the two men, who had died because they could not speak each other's language.

At this point in his story, the Flemish captain fell silent for a few moments, staring into the fire.

The trader poured more wine for his guests, and long into the night, they continued to listen to the Flemish captain's stories of distant voyages, desert islands, gigantic trees, storms, dead calms, and mysterious peoples.

The following day, the Knight told the trader that he wanted to continue by sea to Denmark.

'We're in November now,' said the trader, 'and it's getting colder by the day. People say we're in for a harsh winter. I don't think it will be easy to find a ship to take you home. No sailor would risk travelling north for fear of the cold and of possible storms.'

This news greatly troubled the Knight. At first, he refused to accept his host's advice and tramped the city of Antwerp, speaking to captains and to shipowners, but the answer was always the same.

'At this time of year, and with such a harsh

winter in prospect, no ship would dare to venture so far north.'

On the night of the third day, after supper, when the two men were sitting by the fire, the trader poured his guest a glass of wine and said: 'I have a proposal to make. I can see that you enjoy travelling and adventures, and I need men prepared to travel the world. My business is expanding by the day, and I could do with an associate to help me. This is the age of the navigator, a new era has begun, and enterprising men can now earn vast fortunes. Join me. You will sail in my ships, and perhaps one day you will even voyage in one of those Portuguese caravels to those new lands in the south.'

But the Knight shook his head and answered: 'I find all those tales of the sea, of islands and unknown peoples and distant lands truly marvellous, but I promised that I would be home this Christmas. I will make the journey over land and I will leave tomorrow.'

'It will be a hard journey,' said the trader.

And so it proved. The rivers were frozen, the land covered in snow. It grew colder and colder and the days shorter and shorter. The paths seemed endless. At night, in the inns where he slept, the Knight would dream of those palaces in Venice, of the statues in Florence, and imagine naked tribesmen from the coasts of Africa emerging out of the snowy fields, surrounding him and preventing him from continuing on his way.

Then he would wake with a start, and it seemed to him that all the forces in the world were conspiring to keep him from his home and his people. In the morning, though, he would set off again.

He travelled for long weeks, and because the days were short and it wasn't safe to travel at night, he made very slow progress. He wrapped himself in the fur-lined cloak he had bought in Antwerp, but even then the cold froze him to the bone.

Finally, two days before Christmas, late one afternoon, he reached a small village just a few miles from his own forest. There he was received with great joy by his friends, who, after his long absence, had assumed he was lost. One of them put him up in his house and lent him a horse, because the Knight's horse was exhausted and lame. The Knight asked for news of those he had left behind.

'They're all eagerly waiting for you, but are greatly concerned that you have still not returned and are praying for your safe arrival home,' said a friend.

And very early the next day, the pilgrim left.

It was 24th December, one of the shortest days of the year, and he was riding as fast as he could, wanting to make the most of the few hours of daylight.

By midnight, he must, without fail, reach his house in the clearing surrounded by birch trees.

And when he had travelled a couple of miles, confident now of arriving in time, he entered the great forest. His joy at finding himself so close to his nearest and dearest made him forget his weariness and the cold.

Now, though, after almost two years away, the forest seemed to him both fantastical and strange. Everything was still and silent and waiting. And the silence and the solitude seemed to him frightening and confusing.

The winter had stripped the trees of all their leaves, and their bare branches stood out black or grey or slightly red. Only the pine trees were still green. They were spruce trees, the kind that grow in the north, and which are broad at the base and pointed at the top, their branches beginning at ground level and growing up to form a cone shape as they rise to the sky.

The snow had erased all trails, all tracks, and the Knight was trying to find his way through that labyrinth of trees. His plan was to arrive before nightfall at a small settlement of woodmen close to the river that passed by his house. Once he had found that river, even at night, he couldn't possibly get lost, because the frozen river would guide him.

As he advanced, his ears became accustomed to the silence and he began to distinguish the different rustlings and creakings: a squirrel leaping from branch to branch, or a fox fleeing through the snow. Then, in the distance, he spotted a deer. He was heading east, and after another hour, he came across the tracks left by sledges.

'A good sign,' he thought. 'I'm heading in the right direction now.'

Indeed, by following those tracks, he soon arrived at the small settlement.

All doors were flung wide, and the men of the forest immediately recognized the Knight and greeted him warmly.

He went into the largest of the cabins and sat down by the fire, while the villagers served him bread and honey and hot milk.

'We were beginning to think you would never come back,' said an old man with a long beard.

'I stayed away far longer than I intended,' said the pilgrim Knight. 'But I have, thank God, arrived in time. By midnight tonight, I should be in my own house.'

'It's very late,' said the old man, 'there's more snow on the way, and you can't possibly ride in the dark.'

'I was born in the forest,' said the Knight. 'I know every path. If I follow the river, I won't get lost.'

'The forest is vast and no one will recognize you in the dark. Stay here with us and spend the night in my cabin. Tomorrow, at first light, you can continue on your way.'

'No, I can't,' said the Knight. 'I promised I would be home tonight.'

'The forest is full of starving wolves. What will you do if a pack of wolves attacks you?'

The Knight smiled and answered: 'Have you forgotten that, on Christmas Eve, no wild beast will attack a man?'

And with that, he stood up, said goodbye to the woodmen, mounted his horse and continued on his way.

He headed to his left, in search of the frozen river. However, as soon as the village was out of sight, the snow began to fall so thick and fast that he could barely see.

'I must hurry,' he was thinking, 'I must reach the river as quickly as I can.'

And pulling his hood further down over his eyes, he rode on.

The river still did not appear, and the night was growing ever darker.

He stopped and listened.

'The sensible thing would be to turn back,' he thought. 'But if I don't arrive today, my wife, my children and my servants will think I've died or lost my way in some foreign land. They will spend Christmas in a state of sadness and affliction. I must reach them tonight.'

And so on he rode.

Now, there was not the slightest sound, not even a branch snapped. The squirrels, the foxes and the deer were all hiding in their lairs. The falling snow seemed to multiply the silence.

And the river appeared to have vanished.

'Perhaps I mistook the path,' thought the Knight. 'I'll head in a different direction.'

And he veered a little more to the left.

But it continued to grow dark, the snow continued to fall, the silence continued to grow, and still there was no meeting between man and river.

And gradually it grew darker still.

The hours passed one by one and the lost Knight advanced through the darkness.

However tightly he wrapped his cloak about him, the air froze him to the bone, and his hands began to freeze.

He had lost all notion of how long he had been travelling, and the forest was like an endless labyrinth where the paths went in circles, intersecting and then vanishing.

'I'm lost,' he murmured.

Then the darkness filled with tiny points of bright, reddish light.

The eyes of wolves.

The Knight could hear their light steps in the snow, could feel their hot, hungry breath, could sense the cruel white of their sharp teeth.

Out loud he said: 'Tonight, Christmas Eve, is a night of truce.'

And at the sound of those words, the eyes withdrew and disappeared.

Further on, he heard the roar of a bear.

The Knight reined in his horse, and the bear approached. It stood up on its hind legs and placed its front paws on the horse's neck.

The man could hear the bear breathing, feel its fur on his hand, and see, only inches away, the glint of those small, fierce eyes.

And out loud he said: 'Tonight, Christmas Eve, is a night of truce.'

Then the beast lumbered off, growling.

And the Knight continued on through the silence and the darkness.

He was riding now with no fixed direction, borne along on hope alone, because he could neither hear nor see anything. The branches brushed his face, and he rode aimlessly on.

The horse kept sinking into the snow and so could advance only slowly. Then suddenly it stopped. The man dug in his spurs, but the horse remained stiff and motionless.

'This is the night when I will die,' thought the Knight.

Then he remembered the great blue Jerusalem night all embroidered with stars. And he remembered Balthasar, Gaspar and Melchior, who had read the sky as they travelled. The sky here was dark, hidden, heavy with silence. Not a voice, not a sign of life, but it was to that dark, mute sky that the Knight prayed.

He said the prayer of the Angels, that great shout of joy, trust and kinship that, one night, long, long ago, had pierced the transparent Judean sky.

The words rose up one by one in the pure snowy silence: 'Glory be to God in the highest and peace on earth to all men and women of good will.'

Then, in the distance, among the dark mass of trees, he began to make out a faint glow.

'Thank God,' murmured the Knight. 'It must be a bonfire. It must be some woodman who is as lost as I am and has lit a fire. My prayer was heard. Beside a fire and with my fellow man I will be able to wait for dawn to come.'

The horse neighed. It, too, had seen the light. And gathering together all their strength, man and beast again began to advance.

The light continued to grow brighter, and as it did, from the ground up to the sky, it began to take on the shape of a cone.

It was a great radiant triangle, the top of which rose up above all the other trees.

Now the whole forest was alight. The ice glittered, the snow revealed its whiteness, the air was full of multicoloured reflections, great rays of light shone among the branches and tree trunks.

'What a marvellous bonfire,' he thought. 'I've never seen a more beautiful bonfire.'

But when he reached that bright light, he saw that it wasn't a bonfire, for there, in that clearing surrounded by birch trees, stood his house. And beside the house, the great dark spruce, the largest tree in the forest, was covered in lights, for the Christmas Angels had decorated it with dozens of tiny stars to guide the Knight.

This story, passed on down the generations, became known throughout the North. And that is why, on Christmas Eve, we decorate our Christmas tree with lights.

THE BRONZE BOY

I

The Flowers

Once upon a time there was a marvellous garden full of huge lime trees, birches, oaks, magnolias and plane trees.

There were also rose gardens and orchards, flower beds edged with box, and very long paths flanked by walls of clipped camellia bushes.

There was a hothouse full of maidenhair ferns and other extraordinary plants, each of which had a metal tag attached, bearing the plant's Latin name.

There was a big park, full of very tall plane trees, lakes, grottoes and wild strawberries. And there was a wheat field, full of poppies, and a pine wood in which heathers and ferns grew beneath the mimosas and the pines.

In one of the box-lined borders, there was a bed of gladioli.

Now, gladioli are very snooty flowers, and those gladioli were firmly of the view that their part of the garden was the most elegant spot in which to live.

'All civilised gardens,' they said, 'have box hedges.'

Close to the gladioli stood a pergola covered in wisteria and furnished with tiled benches.

'All the oldest gardens,' said the gladioli, 'have tiled benches.'

When they heard this, the box hedges smiled and murmured in a boxy voice, which is small and moist and green: 'In the old gardens, there were box hedges and tiled benches, but no gladioli.'

The box family is a very ancient one, whereas the gladiola family only came into fashion in the last thirty years.

The gladioli, however, loved being gladioli and thought they were superior to almost all the other flowers.

According to them, roses were sentimental and old-fashioned, and carnations smelled of dentists. They scorned poppies and sunflowers, which grow wild. And as for the flowers on the heather or the gorse bushes that sprang up in the pine wood, the gladioli didn't even consider them to be flowers.

'They're more a kind of prickly weed,' they said.

And while the gladioli did secretly admire the camellias, they didn't really respect them, finding them strange and irritating. Camellias are very different from gladioli: they're vague and dreamy, distant and not in the least bit snooty. Their flowers are always half-hidden away among their hard, glossy leaves. However, one thing the gladioli did admire about camellias was their lack of scent, because, among flowers, having no scent shows great originality.

The flowers for which the gladioli felt genuine respect were the exotic flowers in the hothouse, the ones that had their names written on a metal label attached to them with a piece of raffia.

Unfortunately, the hothouse flowers rarely came out, because they were afraid of catching a cold. At night, when the other flowers went for a stroll, the hothouse flowers stayed at home. Only very occasionally, in August, did they venture forth. However, when they didn't come out, they did receive visitors. And the gladioli would often go to visit them at night. The next day, they would tell the box hedges: 'Yesterday, I went to visit my friend Orchid and my dear friend Begonia.'

The box hedges would titter and make fun, but they spoke in such a faint little murmur that the gladioli, who always talk in loud, strident voices, didn't even hear them and so failed to realise that the box hedges were making fun of their snooty view of life.

The flowers that the gladioli really loved, the flowers for whom they felt unbounded admiration, were the tulips. The gladioli felt almost subservient to them and even set aside their own vanity. In the winter, when the gardener was planting out the tulip bulbs, he would say: 'In shops in the city, a dozen tulips would cost you a fortune.'

In the heart of a gladiola, though, a tulip was worth far more.

'They're a lot of hard work, tulips,' the gardener would say, as he crouched humbly on the dark earth in which the tulip bulbs would germinate.

And the only sadness in the life of the gladioli was that they were not tulips, because tulips are expensive, rare and extremely well-dressed. Their shape is simple, exact and clear. Their colours rich and sumptuous. Their petals are better tailored and better arranged than those of any other flower in the garden. Besides, tulips are the direct descendants of the Dutch tulips grown by the Prince of Orange.

And that is something the gladioli never forget.

There was one flower, though, whom the gladioli loathed, and that was the Lily of the Valley.

The Lily of the Valley is a flower that likes to hide away. She's a very small, white flower and has a marvellous perfume more beautiful even than that of tuberoses.

During the winter, she sleeps beneath the earth under the fallen leaves of the trees. She sleeps the sleep of the dead. In spring, though, her green leaves pierce the earth and grow until they're about a span high. Then, very slowly, the leaves open to reveal, to the astonished light of day, their airy, white, dancerly flowers. And the afternoon breeze takes the perfume of the Lily of the Valley and carries it off, scattering it about the whole garden.

Then the entire garden trembles, and the lofty lime trees and the ancient oaks and the new-born flowers and the lawns and the butterflies all say: 'It's spring! It's spring!'

Only the gladioli are unhappy and say: 'What a show-off! She pretends to hide, pretends to be so simple and humble, pretends to want to remain unseen, but then transforms herself into a perfume that spreads throughout the entire garden!'

And at night, when they go to visit the begonias

and the orchids in the hothouse, the gladioli close the door behind them so as not to be able to smell the scent of the Lily of the Valley.

II

The Gladiola

Now, one day, a gladiola was born who was even snootier than all the other gladioli.

When this gladiola was just unfurling his first flower, the gardener was picking some other gladioli.

'We're going to a party,' said the gladioli he had picked, and who were now lying in a bunch in a basket.

'How wonderful!' said the Gladiola.

And those were his very first words.

As soon as the gardener had gone off with his basket full of cut gladioli, the Gladiola looked at himself and thought: 'I'm a very handsome gladiola!'

Then he looked at the other plants and said: 'Hello, dear friends.'

'Hello, hello,' answered the flowers and the plants.

'Gladioli,' said the wisteria, 'are obviously in fashion. They're always being picked, more often even than the roses or the carnations. We're never picked, of course, because it's so difficult to fit us in a vase.'

From then on, the Gladiola understood that there were two kinds of flower: those who are picked and those who aren't. And he thought: 'How lucky I am to be gladiola! How lucky I am to be in fashion! How lucky that one day I, too, will be picked!'

And he carefully smoothed his petals.

A few days later, the Gladiola suffered a grave disappointment. The lady of the house came into the garden one morning and said to the gardener, who was busy pruning the box hedges: 'Don't pick any more gladioli this year. I'm sick of them. Every party I go to, I see nothing but gladioli.'

'Fine,' said the gardener. 'I won't pick any more gladioli this year.'

'How sad, how annoying, what bad luck!' thought the furious Gladiola.

He decided to seek consolation.

That night, he went to the hothouse to visit the Orchid and the Begonia, having gone there the night before to say goodbye.

With a very grand air, he had announced: 'Dear

friends, I have come to say goodbye because I believe that tomorrow I will be picked.'

So the Begonia and the Orchid were very surprised when they saw him enter the hothouse.

'So you weren't picked after all,' they said.

'No, the lady of the house thinks that we gladioli are too important to the garden and so has ordered the gardener not to pick us any more.'

'Excellent,' said the Orchid, 'we would have missed you so much.'

'We were missing you already,' said the Begonia.

'Thank you, thank you, my friends,' said the Gladiola.

'And would it actually be a good thing to be picked?' said the Orchid.

Then the three launched into a very long, very philosophical discussion, but reached no conclusion at all.

Finally, weary of philosophical debates, the Gladiola said goodbye. He walked along the paths in the moonlight. Deep in his heart, he was still very sad not to have been picked. He walked past the house and stopped.

'I'm going to take a peek inside,' he thought. 'According to the gardener, they have visitors tonight.'

And he went over to a very ancient oak, whose huge branches almost touched the walls of the house.

Music was drifting out through the brightly lit, open windows, spreading and floating through the garden like a perfume.

'Hello, Gladiola,' said the Oak, 'so they haven't picked you yet, then?'

'No,' said the Gladiola, 'I can't be picked. I'm needed in the garden.'

'Did you come to have a peek at the party?' asked the Oak.

'Yes, but I can't see much from down here.'

'If you like, you can sit on one of my branches,' said the Oak.

'Thank you,' said the Gladiola, 'I accept your kind invitation.'

Then with one of his branches, the Oak picked him up from the ground and placed him among the leaves right opposite an open window.

Inside, he could see men all in black and ladies in pale silks, with earrings in their ears and necklaces about their necks. And they were all laughing, talking and dancing.

'Such luxury, such elegance, such wealth!' cried the Gladiola.

'You know,' said the Oak, 'I'm very old now and I've been standing opposite this window for so many years and have seen so many parties that nothing amazes me any more.'

'Do you know the people in there?'

'Yes, I know nearly all of them.'

At this point, a young man and a dark-haired woman wearing a yellow satin dress appeared on the balcony.

'Who are they?' asked the Gladiola.

'She's the best-dressed, most elegant person in the place. A kind of tulip. He, on the other hand, is a snob.'

'What's a snob?' asked the Gladiola.

'A kind of Gladiola.'

'What do snobs do?'

'They have lots of friends and are often invited to people's houses, which is precisely why they're so often invited to other people's houses.'

'What an extraordinary life!' sighed the Gladiola.

The lady and the snob disappeared, and, for a few moments, the balcony remained empty.

Then, the snob reappeared, this time with two different ladies, one on either arm, one wearing a lilac-coloured dress, while the other was tall and thin and dressed in black.

'Who are they?' asked the Gladiola eagerly.

'They're foreigners,' said the Oak, 'the one in lilac is English and a kind of Begonia; the one in black is American and a kind of Orchid. She's filthy rich and has a house all made of glass like a hothouse and she knows snobs all over the world.'

'They look very interesting,' said the Gladiola.

And as the evening wore on, more people came out onto the balcony and the Gladiola always asked: 'Who are they? Who are they?'

And the Oak would explain.

Until, at last, the people left and the music stopped and the rooms emptied and one by one the lights went out.

'I have an idea!' said the Gladiola.

'What's that?' asked the Oak.

'I'm going to give a party!'

'A party?'

'Yes, a party for flowers just like these parties for people. I'm going to give a party at night here in the garden.'

'Well, it's an idea, I suppose,' said the Oak glumly, because he was old and disliked novelties.

'It will be a wonderful party!' promised the Gladiola.

'Possibly. But first you need to ask the Bronze

Boy for his permission.'

'That's true. I'll go and speak to him now. Can you put me down on the ground again?'

The Oak did as asked and the Gladiola set off.

Because the night, you see, is different from the day.

During the day, the flowers are tethered to the earth and cannot move, but the night sets the flowers free. And at night, the flowers can dance and walk about. And while the lady of the house and the gardener were in charge of the garden by day, at night, it was the Bronze Boy.

Between the rose garden and the park, in a shady, solitary, verdant spot, there was another small garden overhung by the branches of very tall trees. In the middle of that garden was a round pond, which was always full of leaves. In the centre of the pond was a tiny island made of rocks and planted with ferns. And in the centre of the island was the statue of a boy made of bronze.

During the day, the Bronze Boy couldn't move and had to keep very still, frozen in the same position, because he was a statue. But at night, he could talk, walk, move and dance, and he was the one who ruled over the garden, the park, the pine wood, the orchard and the wheatfield. And all the trees and all the plants obeyed him because he was the lord of the garden and the king of the night.

'Hello,' said the Bronze Boy when he saw the Gladiola. 'What are you doing in this solitary part of the garden?'

'I need to ask you a favour. I want you to give me permission to organise a party, here in the garden, a party for flowers just like the parties they hold for people.'

'Like the parties they hold for people? But whatever for? We don't need parties. For us, everything is a party: the morning dew is a party, the sunlight is a party, the evening breeze is a party, the dark night is a party. Flowers don't need more parties. Nor do I.'

'It's just to have a bit of fun,' said the Gladiola.

'We're not people,' said the Bronze Boy. 'We don't need to have fun.'

'But you see, no one picked me,' said the Gladiola, 'and I want to go to a party. I need a party.'

'Ah, Gladiola,' said the Bronze Boy, 'you're just like the lady of the house. She doesn't know how to simply stroll in the garden or enjoy the evening breeze or look up at the stars in the night sky. All she wants are parties with lots of people and lots of noise. When she's alone, she withers and fades!'

'If I don't get to go to a party, I'll be very unhappy! Please, let me put on a party.'

Then the Bronze Boy saw how sad and downcast the Gladiola was and took pity on him, saying: 'Don't be sad. Straighten your petals. You shall have a party.'

'Oh, thank you, thank you, thank you, Bronze Boy,' said the Gladiola, bowing. 'I'll start to organise it right away. I'll get an organising committee together. Can we hold the party the night after tomorrow?'

'You can,' said the Bronze Boy. 'It's a full moon that night.'

'Thank you,' said the Gladiola. 'I'd better rush. I have a lot to do.'

And he hurried off along the paths.

On the way, he met the wind.

'Wind,' he said, 'I'm in a hurry. Take me to the hothouse.'

And the wind picked up the Gladiola and carried him through the air to the door of the hothouse.

'Can you push open the door for me,' said the Gladiola.

The wind pushed open the door, and the Gladiola flew inside. Then the wind left, and the door creaked shut of its own accord.

'What's wrong?' asked the Begonia.

'What's happened?' asked the Orchid.

'I bring news!' cried the Gladiola.

And he told them everything.

The Begonia and the Orchid were thrilled.

And the three of them immediately started discussing the details of the party. They agreed that there should be an 'Organising Committee', and there followed a long discussion about who should be part of that Committee. After an hour, they had drawn up this list:

ORGANISING COMMITTEE FOR THE GRAND BALL FOR FLOWERS
GLADIOLA
ORCHID
BEGONIA
TULIP
CARNATION
ROSE

The Gladiola didn't want to include the Rose, because she thought her a very old-fashioned flower. However, the Begonia and the Orchid both declared that they absolutely had to include the Rose on the Committee.

They then agreed to hold a meeting of the six Committee members the following night in the Bronze Boy's garden in order to sort out all the arrangements for the party.

The Gladiola was charged with sending a message to the Tulip, the Carnation and the Rose.

And since it was already growing late, he said goodbye to his friends in the hothouse and returned to his box-hedge border.

III

Florinda

The following morning, the Gladiola summoned three butterflies and asked them to take a message from him to the Tulip, the Carnation and the Rose.

'Tell them from me that we're organising a big party and that they're all members of the Organising Committee, which is why I'm asking them to come to the Bronze Boy's garden tonight.'

The three butterflies flew off with the message, but visited many flowers on the way, and told them about the party too. The garden was soon filled with flowery conversations.

And the butterflies, even giddier than usual,

flew all over the place because flowers kept calling to them, asking: 'Come over here, Butterfly. Tell me the news.'

And the butterflies would stop and tell them the news, flying hither and thither. Finally, though, they reached their destination.

The Tulip, the Carnation and the Rose accepted the invitation and promised to meet that night in the Bronze Boy's garden.

The Gladiola spent a very agitated day. The butterflies kept flying in with messages from the other flowers.

'The Wisteria is very shocked not to be included on the Committee,' said one butterfly.

'The Gypsophila wants to know if she will be invited,' said another butterfly.

The Gladiola sent charming messages to all his acquaintances.

He was extremely excited and swayed back and forth on his stem as if it were a windy day. Impatiently imagining a thousand possible plans, he shook his orange flowers, and the earth securing his root seemed to cut into him like a tight manacle.

At last, night fell.

The Gladiola set off.

He called to the wind to carry him through the

air, but the wind had gone off into the mountains.

It was a tranquil blue night, and the stars were shining down on the great dark trees.

The Gladiola was the first to arrive at the Bronze Boy's garden.

'So how's the party coming along?' asked the Bronze Boy.

'We already have an Organising Committee.'

'Excellent.'

'The weather is perfect. I couldn't find so much as a breath of wind to bring me here.'

'You'll have a marvellous night for your party,' said the Bronze Boy.

Moments later, the Carnation and the Rose arrived.

'Good evening,' they said.

'Good evening,' said the Bronze Boy and the Gladiola.

Immediately afterwards, the Orchid and the Begonia arrived.

'Good evening,' said the Gladiola. 'The only one missing now is the Tulip.'

'Oh, the Tulip is always late,' said the Carnation.

'I hope she got the right message. Butterflies can be so silly!' said the Gladiola anxiously, peering into the shadows.

'I can hear footsteps,' said the Carnation.

But it was just the sound of fallen leaves being blown across the lawn.

'There must have been some mix-up,' sighed the Gladiola.

'The Tulip is always late, but she does arrive eventually. Don't worry,' said the Rose.

Finally, the Tulip arrived.

'I'm so sorry,' she said, 'I was waiting for the night wind to give me a lift, but it never turned up. That's why I'm late.'

'That's fine, my dear friend,' said the Gladiola. 'It doesn't matter. Let's begin the meeting. I think the first problem is deciding which families should be invited. I have a list of forty families.'

'I have only thirty-six on my list,' said the Tulip.

The Carnation and the Rose were shocked, because what the flowers mean by families are the different species: the violets belong to the violet family, the daisies to the daisy family, the roses to the rose family.

'I don't understand,' said the Carnation.

'Neither do I!' said the Bronze Boy.

'I assumed we would invite all the flowers,' said the Rose.

'We have to choose the prettiest, the most

famous, the best-quality flowers,' said the Tulip.

'All flowers are pretty,' said the Bronze Boy.

'But some flowers aren't really flowers,' said the Gladiola.

'All flowers are flowers,' retorted the Bronze Boy angrily.

'You mean that Heather and Gorse are flowers too?' asked the Begonia.

'Of course Heather and Gorse are flowers,' said the Bronze Boy, 'wonderful flowers, because all flowers are wonderful. The flowers of the Heather and the Tuberose, say, are very different, but that's what makes the world so pretty. I am the king of the garden, and I want all the flowers to be invited.'

The Gladiola sighed and said: 'The next problem is where to hold the party.'

'Here?' said the Carnation.

'It's a bit out of the way,' said the Begonia.

'And a bit gloomy,' said the Tulip.

'In the hothouse?' suggested the Orchid.

'Too hot and stuffy,' said the Carnation.

'In the rose garden?' suggested the Rose.

'On the tennis courts?' suggested the Gladiola.

'Ah,' said the Carnation, 'I have an idea. Why not in the Glade of Plane Trees?'

This was in the middle of the park. It was a

marvellous place, a vast round area surrounded by very tall trees. At one end was a small oval lake and beside the lake was a romantic pergola.

All around, in the shade of the plane trees, stood old stone benches covered in moss. And in the middle of the glade was a large stone vase that had once been filled with soil and plants. The plants had withered and died, though, and the gardener had emptied the vase and it now stood empty.

Everyone agreed that the glade was the ideal spot.

'The third thing we need to agree on,' said the Gladiola, 'is the orchestra.'

'Frogs,' said the Begonia.

'Cuckoos and woodpeckers,' said the Carnation.

'Nightingales,' said the Rose.

'Blackbirds, gadflies and toads,' said the Carnation.

'I think it would be best if they all sang together. That would make a really magnificent orchestra,' said the Gladiola.

The Committee agreed.

'Now,' the Gladiola went on, 'we have to agree how to decorate the room.'

'It isn't a room,' said the Carnation.

'All right, we have to agree on how to decorate

the glade,' said the Gladiola.

'We don't need to decorate it,' said the Bronze Boy. 'The trees and the stars don't need decoration.'

'I have an idea, though,' said the Tulip.

'What's that?' said the Bronze Boy.

'We could put a string of glow-worms around the lake.'

'Yes, I agree,' said the Bronze Boy.

'And what should we put in the stone vase? It can't stay empty. An empty vase looks ugly,' said the Orchid.

'Hm,' said the Rose.

'Hm,' said the Gladiola.

'Hm,' said the Begonia.

'Hm,' said the Carnation.

'You usually put flowers in a vase,' said the Tulip.

'Flowers!' shrieked the Rose indignantly. '*We* are flowers.'

'This isn't a party for people, it's a party for flowers,' cried a very angry Carnation.

'But you have to put something in a vase. A vase can't just be empty,' retorted the Tulip.

'I know,' said the Bronze Boy, 'if, at a party for people, people put flowers in vases, then at a party for flowers, the flowers should put people in vases.'

'How?' said the Gladiola.

'We need a person to put in the stone vase,' concluded the Bronze Boy.

'But who?' asked the Rose.

'A person who resembles a flower,' answered the Bronze Boy.

'They don't exist,' said the Rose.

'We could put the lady of the house in there,' suggested the Gladiola.

'She looks more like a deer than a flower,' said the Carnation.

'What about the master of the house, then?' said the Begonia.

'He looks like a turkey. No use at all,' said the others.

'And the daughter of the lady of the house?' asked the Orchid.

'No, no,' said the Rose. 'She looks like a plastic rose.'

'I know a really elegant lady who resembles a Tulip,' said the Gladiola. 'I saw her yesterday at the party. She would look very good in a vase, except I don't know where she lives.'

'I,' said the Bronze Boy, 'know someone who is just like a flower.'

'Who's that?' asked the flowers.

'Florinda.'

'Yes, yes, we love Florinda,' said the Rose, the Carnation, the Begonia, the Tulip, the Orchid and the Gladiola.

Because all the flowers adored Florinda.

Florinda was seven years old and the daughter of the gardener. And she resembled all the flowers. Her hair was golden like the Sunflower's petals, her blue eyes were like two violets, her slender, white hands were like camellias, her soft, young skin like a rose and her red lips like a carnation.

'We're all agreed then and it's all arranged,' said the Gladiola.

The flowers said goodbye to the Bronze Boy and went off laughing and dancing through the moonlight and past the other garden flowers.

IV

The Party

The following day, when darkness had fallen, a nightingale began to sing outside Florinda's window.

And Florinda woke, shaking her head and rubbing her eyes, and said: 'How beautifully that nightingale sings!'

'Florinda,' said the nightingale, 'would you like to come to a marvellous party?'

'I would,' said Florinda.

'Then come with me.'

Florinda jumped out of bed and climbed out of the window where the nightingale was waiting for her.

They crossed the orchard and a wood and reached the outskirts of the park.

The shadows of the trees met and mingled in the air above.

'I think I'm a little bit afraid,' murmured Florinda.

'Don't be afraid. I'll look after you,' said a voice beside her.

Florinda turned and saw a tall, green, handsome boy.

'Oh!' she said. 'You're the Bronze Boy. I thought you couldn't speak, I thought you were a statue.'

'By day, I'm a statue,' said the Boy. 'But by night, I'm a person and the king of the garden.'

'In that case,' said Florinda, 'take me with you to see the party.'

And they went together through the park and reached the glade.

'This is where the party is,' said the Bronze Boy, 'but it hasn't yet started.'

The lake was already surrounded by glow-worms.

'How lovely!' said Florinda. 'They've put a necklace of lights around the lake!'

'Your place is over there,' said the Bronze Boy, pointing to the stone vase.

'Why there?' she asked.

'Because you look like a flower.'

Florinda laughed and said: 'Then put me in the vase.'

And the Bronze Boy picked her up in his arms, placed her in the vase, then sat down beside her.

'Is the party going to begin?' asked Florinda.

'Yes,' he said.

At a gesture from him, the nightingales and the woodpeckers, the frogs, the toads and the gadflies, and the blackbirds and the cuckoos all began to sing.

Then the Gladiola appeared on the edge of the clearing.

And seeing the Gladiola walking towards her, Florinda sighed and said: 'The night is so amazing and so different!'

'The night,' said the Bronze Boy, 'is our day, the day of things, of flowers, plants and statues. By day, we're motionless, imprisoned. By night, though, we're free and that's when we dance.'

The Gladiola stopped in the middle of the glade opposite the stone vase and bowed.

'Hello, Gladiola,' said Florinda, 'I'm so pleased to see you walking about like a person.'

'And I,' said the Gladiola, bowing again, 'am very pleased to see you sitting in a vase like a flower.'

'Oh, look, look,' said Florinda, pointing.

The Roses and the Carnations had arrived, and they were immediately followed by the Daisies, the Narcissi, the Lilies, the Poppies, the Forget-me-nots, the Sunflowers, the Camellias, the Heathers, the Marguerites, the Pansies and the Wisteria.

The hothouse flowers arrived shortly afterwards.

The Gladiola danced with the Begonia.

The Tulip had not yet arrived.

Florinda sat on the edge of the vase, laughing and clapping her hands for joy.

The dances of the flowers were extraordinary, very light and slow.

First, the flowers formed a big circle. Then, the circle broke up and changed into a star shape. And Florinda, in her vase, was the centre of the circle and the centre of the star. As the star turned lightly, slowly, it split into many stars. Then each star became a new shape, a circle or a lozenge or some still more complicated shape. And each time a new shape appeared, Florinda would say: 'Ah!'

And the Bronze Boy told her the different names of the shapes.

Finally, still slowly turning, the flowers again formed into a big circle, and the dance ended.

More and more flowers kept appearing out of the darkness.

But the Tulip had still not yet appeared.

'These flower dances are extraordinary and so different,' said Florinda. 'I had no idea that flowers could dance. They teach me many things at school, but they've never taught me that.'

'That's because they don't know. Very few people know these things.'

'I see,' said Florinda.

And a new dance began.

The Gladiola didn't join in, though, because he was concerned that the Tulip had still not arrived. He leaned against the stone vase to watch the dancing.

'Why aren't you dancing?' asked the Bronze Boy.

'I'm worried. The Tulip hasn't arrived yet, and

I'm afraid something might have happened to her.'

'Just be patient. Nothing will have happened to her. You know perfectly well that the Tulip always arrives late.'

And at the end of the third dance, the Tulip arrived.

She looked lovely, tall and erect, with her yellow dress all smooth and shining.

The Gladiola rushed to meet her and asked her to come and dance with him.

But the Tulip said she didn't want to dance and went and stood by the edge of the lake, where she watched her own golden reflection bobbing on the water by the light of the glowworms.

Other flowers invited her to dance too, but she always refused. And the flowers went away.

Only the Gladiola stayed by her side, chatting to her, although the Tulip barely heard him, being too busy gazing at her reflection in the water.

'You know,' Florinda was saying to the Bronze Boy, 'there's a lime tree opposite my window, and, in the summer, when I sleep with the window open, just before I fall asleep, I look out at the lime tree and I see the leaves dancing, and I see them signalling to each other and I hear them talking and murmuring secrets. But when I tell other people about this the next day, they all say: leaves don't talk and don't send signals either. It's just the wind stirring the leaves.'

'Florinda,' said the Bronze Boy, 'I'm going to tell you a big secret: when you see something, believe it, even if everyone else says it's not true.'

The Lily of the Valley, so small and white and light as the breeze, danced every dance. And her bell-shaped flowers swayed, perfuming the night.

'If I were a flower,' Florinda said, 'I would like to be a Lily of the Valley, hidden among the grass inside two green leaves.'

'The Lily of the Valley,' said the Bronze Boy, 'hides among its leaves so that no one can see her, because she doesn't want to be picked. And yet her perfume fills the air, and people follow that scent and discover her hiding place and pick her.'

Still barely hearing what the Gladiola was saying, the Tulip continued to gaze at herself in the lake. And while she was doing this, she saw a white reflection come dancing over the water to meet her own golden reflection. And at that same moment, she found herself surrounded by an extraordinary perfume. She looked up and saw the Tuberose.

'What a lovely dress you're wearing, Tulip,' said the Tuberose. 'Come and dance with me.'

'I will,' said the Tulip, giddy on his perfume.

'But you said you didn't want to dance!' cried the Gladiola indignantly.

The Tulip didn't even hear him.

All the other flowers were astonished to see the Tulip dancing. She was so tall and erect, and her slender, shiny yellow dress swayed atop her slender stem.

The Gladiola went and leaned on the stone vase, looking rather wounded and lonely.

'It's a lovely party,' Florinda said to him.

'Yes, it was a brilliant idea of yours,' said the Bronze Boy.

'Yes, it's all gone really very well, but I'm worried about the Tulip. I'm afraid that dancing with the Tuberose might be bad for her. The scent of the Tuberose is too strong, it can make you dizzy. She's sure to feel ill at the end of this dance. We scentless flowers are very delicate.'

But the Tulip danced with the Tuberose three times in a row.

At the end of the third dance, though, the Lily of the Valley passed close by.

'What's that perfume?' asked the Tuberose.

'It's the Lily of the Valley,' said the Tulip.

'I've never seen the Lily of the Valley!'

'She's always hidden away among her leaves.'

'I'd really like to see her,' said the Tuberose.

And leaving the Tulip, he went off in pursuit of that perfume.

It was now very late, and the moon had disappeared.

The park surrounding the glade had grown darker, and you could see the stars more clearly.

The Tuberose led the Lily of the Valley to the edge of the lake.

'Before I met you,' he said, 'I thought no other flower could be as highly perfumed as me. Sometimes the evening breeze would bring a little of your perfume to the border where I live, and I would think: "It's the scent of spring", but now that I've met you, I know this marvellous perfume belongs to you not to the spring.'

The Tulip did not dance again. She returned to her place on the other side of the lake. The Gladiola joined her to talk and keep her company, but she barely heard him. She was staring at the shimmering white reflections of the Tuberose and the Lily of the Valley on the other side of the lake, far from her own golden reflection.

'Why did you go and dance with the Tuberose?' asked the Gladiola. 'I find his perfume so cloying!'

But the Tulip didn't even answer.

'This is the loveliest party I've ever been to!' declared Florinda. 'Everything here is so amazing, so different. The flowers are alive: they walk, they talk and they dance. And I am a flower too. I rest my head on the sweetness of the night, and my hands are cool and perfumed. And the Carnation, the Rose, the Water Lily and the Jonquil are saying: "See how pretty Florinda looks in her vase!"'

Suddenly, though, Florinda fell silent, because another voice, loud and clear and confident, was echoing across the park.

Hearing that voice, the flowers all trembled. They stopped dancing and stood utterly motionless.

'It's the cockerel,' said the Bronze Boy. 'It's the cockerel announcing that the night has ended.'

And suddenly, there was general confusion, with the flowers rushing all over the place and spinning on the spot like the leaves in autumn when the wind makes them whirl around on the ground.

And, in an instant, they had all disappeared. The glade was empty.

'Oh,' said Florinda. 'The flowers have run away.'

'The cock crowed. It's nearly dawn,' said the Bronze Boy. 'The flowers have all returned to their beds.'

'What's that star over there, so pretty and so bright?' asked Florinda, pointing up at the sky.

'It's Venus, the morning star.'

'Tell me the stories of the stars,' said Florinda, resting her head on the Boy's shoulder.

But he didn't tell her anything. He could see that Florinda was so worn out she had fallen asleep. Very carefully, he picked her up, lifted her out of the vase and carried her in his arms through the park.

All around them, the first morning mists were rising up from the earth. The dry branches snapped under the Boy's feet. The dark garden was very slowly growing lighter.

They finally reached the gardener's house. The Bronze Boy climbed in through the window and laid the sleeping Florinda on the bed.

'Goodbye, Florinda,' he murmured.

And he climbed back out through the window.

He strode quickly across the garden and the park and returned to his place on the island of ferns and rocks in the middle of the round lake. When the Sun rose, he changed back into a statue.

That morning, Florinda slept until very late. Her mother came to wake her.

'Quick, Florinda, it's time to go to school. Hurry.'

And still half-asleep, Florinda got washed and dressed, drank a glass of milk, snatched up a piece of bread and her satchel and raced off to school.

On the way, she began to remember. She began to remember the party, the Gladiola, the Bronze Boy and all the flowers.

And during class, she didn't even hear what the teacher was saying because she could think only of that wonderful party.

At breaktime, she told all this to her friends, but they said: 'You must have been dreaming. Flowers can't speak or dance, and statues can't move.'

'At night, though, everything's different,' said Florinda.

But her friends just laughed and made fun of her.

Then Florinda began to think that perhaps they were right.

And after school, she went for a walk in the garden and the park.

The flowers were sitting still and silent in their borders, just swaying slightly in the passing breeze.

Florinda went to the round lake. Beneath the great green shadows of the trees, on his island of rocks and ferns, the Bronze Boy stood silent and motionless.

'It's me, Bronze Boy,' she said, 'move, speak.'

But the Bronze Boy neither moved nor spoke.

'Oh,' sighed Florinda, 'I must have been mistaken. It was just a dream after all, and I didn't see the things I saw. Nothing happened. I simply dreamed it!'

And she went home.

Many years passed. Florinda slowly grew up and almost forgot about that fantastic party of flowers.

Then one night after supper, in the year Florinda turned fifteen, her mother said to her: 'Florinda, I need you to run an errand for me. Take this basket over to the cook, will you?'

Florinda took the basket, which was large and very heavy because it was full of eggs, and left the house.

It was the first time her mother had sent her on an errand at that hour, because the gardener's house was on the other side of the park and the wood, and to reach the big house, she would have to cross the wood, the whole park, the orchard and the gardens.

Florinda wasn't afraid though. It was the month of May, and it was a calm, moonlit night.

When she reached the park, she looked up at the great dark trees, full of glimmering lights and tremulous leaves, and she thought: 'It's like a dream.'

And she remembered the party of the flowers.

But she continued on her way and reached the big house and delivered the basket of eggs to the cook. Then she said goodnight and walked slowly back, in no hurry to go home.

The May night with its shadows and its lights, its perfumes, its flowers and its murmurings seemed like some fantastical story. The leaves stirred gently in the breeze and appeared to be conversing with each other.

'Everything seems so alive,' thought Florinda. 'It's as if everything were watching me, listening to me!'

And in her aimless wanderings, she eventually reached the Bronze Boy's garden.

He was standing on his island of rocks and ferns, utterly silent and still.

Florinda stopped.

Everything in the garden seemed to have stopped too. Suddenly even the breeze stopped.

Then the Boy held out one hand and said very slowly: 'Florinda, do you remember me?'

'Oh, yes, of course I remember you!' she answered.

And the Bronze Boy stepped down from his island, jumped over the lake and stood before Florinda.

'Do you remember the party of the flowers and the glade and that spring night?'

'Of course, yes, now I remember everything. But I thought it was all a dream. I thought that everything I'd seen was too extraordinary to be true.'

'Both the extraordinary and the fantastic are true. Because there are two countries, the night is one country and the day is another.'

'What a marvellous place the world is!' said Florinda.

And she gave her hand to the Bronze Boy and together they walked through the garden.

The Forest

I

Once upon a time there was an old country estate entirely surrounded by walls.

The grounds contained groves of wonderful old trees, as well as lakes, streams, gardens, orchards, woods, fields and a large area of parkland, beyond which a pine forest stretched almost to the sea.

The estate lay on the outskirts of the city. You entered through a heavy, green, wrought-iron gate, and the first thing you saw was a large house surrounded by very tall lime trees whose leaves, green on one side and almost white on the other, fluttered in the breeze.

This was the house where Isabel lived.

At the time, Isabel was eleven years old, and so every weekday she would go to school, swinging her satchel full of books, first in one hand, then in the other.

At four o'clock she would come back home, grab something to eat, and rush back outside to play in the garden.

Isabel had no brothers or sisters, so she knew how to play on her own and have conversations with the trees, the stones and the flowers.

Every day she explored the old estate. In autumn, she would gather chestnuts, stamping hard on their spiky green husks to open them. In winter, she would pick violets and camellias. In spring, she would climb up into the cherry trees to eat the very first sweet, dark red cherries. She would climb other trees too, and every year she would find small round birds' nests made of bits of grass, dried leaves and feathers, each nest containing four green and brown speckled eggs. She would walk through the fields of wheat, which undulated like a gentle sea, airy and light. Sometimes she would spend hours reading under the pergola, where the mauve wisteria hung in great perfumed clusters, buzzing with bees. Or she would stroll slowly through the shimmering green of the park, listening to the sound of the plane trees' lofty canopies stirring in the breeze. And she knew the places, hidden among grasses and leaves, where the wild strawberries grew.

Isabel usually played alone, but sometimes she would go and see the old gardener, who was called Tomé and was her best friend. Tomé would teach her the names of the trees and flowers, and Isabel would help him with the weeding and watering. With Tomé, she would also visit the places where she could not go alone – for the door of the greenhouse, the henhouse and the cellar were always locked. The air was hot and humid in the enormous greenhouse, with its roof of whitewashed glass. Inside grew marvellously slender, delicate ferns, purple begonias, speckled-green orchids that looked like poisonous insects, and other plants and flowers whose strange names were written on metal tags tied to their stems with raffia.

In the henhouse, Isabel would scatter the corn, and a gaggle of cackling hens would gather round her. Then she would shout: 'Come on, old turkey!' and, fluffing up his feathers, the turkey would reply: 'Glu, glu, glu'. And there would always be a new brood of yellow and brown chicks to see. Isabel would pick them up very carefully, cupping both hands around the gentle warmth of their feathery bodies, in which quivered a tiny, startled heart.

Then Tomé would take her to the cellar, where

everything was dark. Isabel would shout out: 'Hu!', and dozens of bats would unhook themselves from the walls. Isabel would tie a scarf around her head so that the bats wouldn't get caught in her hair. There were great big wooden racks for ripening apples and pears after they'd been picked, which is why the cellar always smelled of autumn.

Tomé would take the reddest of the apples from the racks and give it to Isabel. The shiny skin crunched between her teeth and, beneath it, the apple's flesh was sweet and cool, firm and white.

Isabel was very familiar with all these marvellous things. Each year brought with it the four seasons. Spring filled the trees with light green leaves and scattered a host of poppies across the fields. Then the swallows would return and flowers would appear everywhere, swaying gently in the invisible breeze. Then came summer, and the days grew longer and the air became heavy with scent, the bees buzzing around the hanging clusters of wisteria. Roses, narcissi, carnations and tulips bloomed in the flower beds. Every morning, the gardener would bring great baskets of fruit to the kitchen: first, there were cherries and strawberries, then peaches, plums and pears. A little later came the figs and grapes. Then autumn would begin. The days became shorter and more golden; the grapes were picked, the first spiky green husks fell from the sweet chestnut trees, there were dahlias and chrysanthemums in the gardens, and the ground was covered in yellowing leaves that, one by one, detached themselves from the lofty branches of the trees and fell slowly, twirling in the air. Suddenly, a keen grey wind would blow through the estate; the furious roar of the sea could be heard in the distance and winter was upon them. It would rain for a week without stopping. When it did stop, the cold would begin. The first camellias, purest white, appeared. Every day was shorter than the one before. The plane trees and lime trees, stripped of their leaves, stretched their bare branches up towards the pale sky. Even the water in the ponds froze, and when Isabel made her way to school in the mornings, the paths were covered in frost.

On rainy winter days, Isabel would spend her afternoons in the house.

Everything in that house was huge: doors, windows, kitchen, pantry, bedrooms, reception rooms, staircases and hallways.

But the biggest room in the house was the great entrance hall, where the Christmas tree would stand. Off this hallway lay the main reception rooms: the dining room with its seemingly endless table; the drawing room where they would have afternoon tea on winter afternoons; the piano room where Isabel would try out, one by one, the mysterious sounds of the black and white keys; the library with its shelves full of leathery books with fusty gold patterns, and a large table on which was placed a globe of the world. Then there was the red drawing-room where visitors were received; the games room where Isabel would build castles out of cards on the green baize table, or use the mahjong and domino pieces to construct wondrous cities inhabited only by the knights from the chess set; and the billiards room where she would play with the red and white ivory balls, trying to roll them into the little net pockets. Most mysterious of all was the ballroom. The house was so big that no one ever went in there. The servants may have cleaned it while Isabel was at school, but, since early childhood, she had only ever seen that room deserted and shuttered.

Sometimes, on rainy afternoons, Isabel would go and explore the ballroom. She would carefully open one of the shutters just a crack, and a thin shaft of sunlight would penetrate the darkness, picking out the furniture covered in white dust sheets, the heavy red damask curtains, the large mirrors liquid as lakes, the marble statues, white, motionless and mute, and the big blue carpet bursting with crimson roses. Over all these objects hovered a deep, somnolent, heavy silence, as if this were Sleeping Beauty's palace. One day, thought Isabel, a knight would come. He would sound his hunting horn and the hooves of his horse would kick up the gravel in the courtyard. Then they would hear the clinking of his silver spurs on the granite steps. And then, all of a sudden, as if touched by lightning, the ballroom would awaken. The piano would begin to play of its own accord, an invisible hand would light all the candles, the white dust sheets would fall from the furniture, and the scent of roses would fill the room. Then, one by one, the statues would smile and step down from their pedestals. But until that day came, she must be patient. The room needed to remain mute, still and solitary, plunged in silence and semi-darkness. So Isabel closed the shutter again, fastened the iron bolt, and, without a sound, tiptoed out of the room.

On the other side of the house were the kitchen, pantry and airing cupboards. Here, all was noise and bustle, with servants coming and going, washing, tidying, cooking and gossiping. On this side of the house the most important person was cook; she was always very busy, surrounded by meat, eggs, vegetables and chickens. In summer, she would stir an enormous pot of strawberry jam. In autumn, she would make slabs of quince jelly, which would be left for several days to dry in the sun on the south-facing verandah. At Christmas, she would roast a huge turkey stuffed with chestnuts and fried cassava, and for Easter there would be roasted goat, seasoned with herbs. She always carried a bunch of keys hanging from her belt, and it was she who reigned over the larder, a dark, mysterious kingdom where the scent of vanilla and cinnamon hung in the air.

Cook had a very bad temper and would spend the whole day grumbling at Emília, the kitchen maid, who peeled the potatoes, washed the pots and plucked the chickens. But when cook was in a good mood, she would give Isabel magnificent presents. Sometimes these took the form of little golden cakes, still warm from the oven or bars of hard cooking chocolate from the larder, or raisins and dried figs.

So Isabel knew all the things in the house: she knew that at Christmas there would always be a pine tree, laden with lights and glass baubles, standing in the middle of the entrance hall. She knew that at Easter there would be painted eggs hidden in the box hedges. And she knew that on her birthday there would be visitors and presents.

'It's two months till Christmas,' she would think.

Or the gardener would say: 'There'll be cherries next month.'

Or: 'There'll be tulips next week.'

But one day something different and extraordinary happened.

II

It was a Saturday afternoon in October, and Isabel didn't have classes on Saturday afternoons.

Therefore, as soon as lunch was over, she went outside to play. The weather was still very warm and not a blade of grass stirred.

Isabel made her way to a small area of woodland close to the house.

It was a very solitary place where no one ever went, not even the gardener, because everything there grew wild and there were no flower beds or even flowers to tend.

The ground was completely covered in moss, and the flickering shade beneath the tall trees was pierced here and there by golden rays of sunshine.

Isabel lay down on the ground next to an oak tree and began to read. After a quarter of an hour, though, she grew bored with the book and put it to one side and began to study a column of ants marching through the moss towards a hole beside the tree. Then Isabel's gaze fell on the trunk of the oak tree. It was huge, dark and gnarled - it would have taken three men to put their arms around it. The exposed roots, sticking out a little above the ground, formed arches and cavities that reminded her of small caves.

'A good place for dwarves to live,' thought Isabel.

She found this thought extraordinarily interesting.

When she was seven years old, soon after learning to read, Isabel had read the story of *Snow White and the Seven Dwarves*. She often thought about this story. It seemed to her that it would be a wonderful thing to live among dwarves! She would imagine where the dwarves lived, in palaces buried in the earth like rabbit warrens, or hidden in solitary places, inside tree trunks.

'I'd like to see a dwarf,' she said to her maid Mariana.

'There are no dwarves, or only in story books,' replied Mariana.

But Isabel did not believe her.

For months she looked for dwarves among the stones and plants and grasses in the park, but she never found any. So she ended up convincing herself that Mariana was right after all.

Now, though, looking at those ancient roots, she was thinking: 'It's a pity there are no dwarves. This would make an excellent house for dwarves.'

And, after a few moments' reflection, she decided to make a tiny little house there and imagine that dwarves would come and live in it.

Using sticks and stones and bits of bark from a plane tree, she built some walls and roofs around the old tree. Then she covered the roofs with moss, so as to shelter the house from the cold and rain. She went to find some reeds and cut them into pieces of equal length with a pair of secateurs, which she asked the gardener if she could borrow. By tying the reeds together with raffia, she made a little front door that could open and close.

She spent the whole afternoon doing this.

The next day was Sunday.

Isabel went up to her doll's house, a birthday present from when she was younger, and took from it a rug, a table, a chair and a bed, along with the mattress, pillow and blankets.

She put everything in a basket, put the basket over her arm, bounded down the stairs four at a time, and rushed into the garden.

When she reached the tree, she knelt down and very carefully, so as not to disturb the roof and walls she had built, lay the rug on the floor of the little house. On the rug, she put the bed, along with the mattress, pillow and blankets. Beside it she placed the table and chair.

Then, with little stones and bits of moss, she plugged all the gaps in the walls and roof.

The house was magnificent. It had a very cosy, welcoming air about it. Someone was bound to want to live in it, tucked in beside the old gnarled tree trunk, or, at the very least, to spend a night there. Isabel wished she was only a few inches tall, so that she herself could fit inside. She gazed at her work for a long time, then sighed: 'What a pity no one lives here!'

And very carefully she closed the reed door she had made the previous day.

Just then she heard voices calling her: 'Isabel, Isabel!'

It was her cousins, who had come to play and

have their afternoon tea with her, as they always did on Sundays.

But Isabel didn't want them to see the little house, afraid they might damage or even destroy it. So she got to her feet, picked up her basket and ran towards the voices. And when she found her cousins, she took them off to the other side of the estate.

III

On Monday, Isabel had a lot of homework to do, and so she couldn't visit the house she had built in the woods. On Tuesday she had to accompany her mother to an aunt's birthday party. On Wednesday she had to go to the dressmaker's.

But Thursday was a holiday.

Isabel got up so early that even the servants weren't all awake.

The kitchen maid, who was always the first person in the house to get up, gave Isabel her cup of hot milk and a piece of bread and honey. Isabel drank down her milk in a single gulp, put on her coat, grabbed the piece of bread and went outside.

The night mist had not yet lifted and everything was wrapped in a thick white cloud. The trees seemed to be floating and the ends of the paths disappeared into nothingness. The air was filled with the delicious smells of autumn, of apples and rosemary.

Isabel ran and skipped her way to the little wood. She was in such a hurry that she even forgot to eat the bread she was holding in her hand. She was filled with a mixture of curiosity and concern that someone might have destroyed her work.

But when she reached the old tree trunk, she beamed. The house was still in one piece, its bark roof neatly covered in moss and its reed door firmly shut. It had an extraordinarily peaceful, comfortable air about it.

Isabel knelt down on the ground and carefully opened the door.

When she looked inside, she froze, speechless, mouth open, eyes wide and hands in the air.

For some moments she was so astonished she could neither move nor take in what she was seeing.

Finally, she slowly rubbed her eyes, then opened them very wide and murmured: 'I must be dreaming!'

For inside the house something truly remarkable and incredible had happened: lying on the bed was a real-life dwarf.

The dwarf was sleeping. And he was sleeping so soundly he was even snoring. His face was red as a strawberry and the tip of his long beard touched the ground.

As well as amazement, Isabel felt a great welling up of happiness and affection. The more she thought about it, the more it seemed to her that she had been waiting for this dwarf her whole life. Finding him here, now, was both extraordinary and perfectly straightforward.

She tried to guess his height, and decided that he must be exactly three inches tall.

'Dwarves are even smaller than I imagined,' she thought.

She was tempted to wake him, because she was very curious to know if he could speak, and, if so, in which language. She feared dwarves might have their own language that she wouldn't be able to understand. She considered gently calling to him: 'Mister Dwarf!'

But she was afraid she might scare him, and so decided to wait until he woke up.

Without making a sound, she lay down on the ground and rested her chin on her hands. It was a comfortable position. She could stay like that for a long time watching him sleep.

The dwarf was covered by the blanket, but the tips of his boots stuck out. His face, which was very red and covered in tiny wrinkles, bore an expression that was at once cheerful and grave. One of his hands lay on top of the blanket, resting on his beard, and on his ring finger shone a tiny gold ring.

Isabel could not stop looking at him.

'What an extraordinary thing!' she thought. 'I made a house for a dwarf that didn't exist, and the dwarf appeared!'

But the moss Isabel was lying on was still damp from the morning dew, and after ten minutes of gazing, she gave a loud sneeze.

It was like a thunderclap.

The dwarf opened his eyes and, seeing Isabel's face pressed almost right up against the door of his house, he was so terrified that he rolled out of bed.

'Don't be afraid! Please don't be afraid!' she implored.

But the dwarf, looking ever more distraught, leapt across to the far side of the bed.

'I won't harm you. Please don't be scared of me,' Isabel begged.

But the dwarf didn't answer her.

He looked around for a hole he could escape through, but she had blocked all the holes with stones and moss. The only way out of that house was through the front door.

Seeing the little man's distress, the girl also began to get upset. She didn't know what to do to reassure him.

She remembered her bread and honey, which she hadn't yet eaten and which was sitting on the ground beside her. She broke off a tiny little corner and held it out to the dwarf, but he shook his head, making it clear that her offer didn't interest him.

Isabel sighed and, after thinking for a few minutes, said this to him: 'Dear, dear dwarf! Please don't be scared of me. I don't want to hurt you. I just want to get to know you. I love dwarves. I've spent my whole life thinking about dwarves. When I was younger, I spent all my afternoons in the park, the woods and the pine forest looking for a dwarf. I searched through the undergrowth and in the hollows of trees, but I never found one. In the end, I had to admit, very reluctantly, that dwarves didn't even exist! But now I've found you, I can see that you do exist, and here we are, looking at each other, right here, right now. But you're afraid of me! Tell me: what do I need to do for you to make peace with me and be my friend?'

'Let me out of here,' replied the dwarf.

His voice was soft, but clear and musical.

'There we are!' Isabel exclaimed. 'How wonderful! You can speak my language!'

'I can speak every language,' replied the little man, somewhat disdainfully.

'I only know Portuguese and French,' said Isabel. 'But I'm only eleven years old. How old are you?'

'Three hundred.'

'How lucky!' exclaimed Isabel, full of amazement. 'You must know lots of things.'

'All dwarves know lots of things,' he said.

'Then tell me a story,' asked Isabel.

But the dwarf shook his head and said: 'Not now. Only when we become friends.'

'What do I have to do for you to be my friend?'

'Let me out of here and go away.'

'If I let you out of here and go away, you'll run off and never come back.'

'That's very true.'

'So what should we do?' she asked.

'Go away so I can get out of here.'

'You're very stubborn and very suspicious,' said Isabel indignantly. 'I always thought dwarves were more intelligent than that. Can't you see that if I wanted to, I could grab you this very instant, put you in my pocket and take you to my house? I haven't done that because I don't want to frighten you and I want you to trust me.'

'If you want me to trust you, then go away and let me leave.'

'Well,' sighed Isabel, 'we clearly can't agree. The best thing would be for us to talk a while and see if your fear goes away. Tell me how you came to be here at my house.'

'Well,' he explained, 'I have many houses. Some are underground, in mysterious places you couldn't even imagine. Others are inside the hollow trunks of old trees and are completely lined with feathers, leaves and bits of dried grass, like birds' nests. My houses are very comfortable and cosy, warm in winter and cool in summer. As you know (or perhaps you don't, since people know so little about us that they think we don't even exist), dwarves sleep during the day and go out at night. Last night, after the moon disappeared just before dawn, I happened to pass by, saw this house of yours and thought it looked very nice. I decided to try out the bed to see if it was comfortable. I lay down and pulled the covers over me. I didn't take off my boots because I wasn't intending to stay. But I was so tired after so much walking that somehow,

I don't know how, I fell asleep.'

'How lucky!'

'Not really,' he replied.

'Don't be afraid, dwarf,' Isabel begged. 'I'm not going to lock you up.'

'Listen,' said the dwarf, 'let's make a pact.'

'Okay, what will it be?'

The little man pointed at a lime tree thirty feet away and said: 'Go and stand by that lime tree and let me leave in peace. Don't come running after me. Then I'll leave, but I will come back.'

'Promise you'll come back?'

'I promise,' he said solemnly.

'I accept your promise.'

Isabel fixed her eyes firmly on the dwarf, then stood up and went over to the lime tree.

As soon as she was a few yards away, the dwarf darted nimbly out of the house. His little body all but disappeared, because as well as being very small, he was wearing a green outfit that blended in perfectly with the leaves and the moss. He ran off behind the tree and disappeared into a clump of reeds.

Isabel stood motionless for several long minutes to see if he would come back, but there was no sign of him.

Isabel went over to the clump of reeds and

called out: 'Dwarf!'

But no one appeared.

Once again she called: 'Dwarf, dwarf! I'm looking for you. Please answer me!'

But no one answered.

Isabel spent a long time looking. She rummaged through the reeds and peered behind all the trees.

She felt sad and disappointed.

Finally, she went to sit beside the oak tree in front of the little house.

She called out very loudly: 'Dwarf, I'm waiting for you.'

She picked up the bread she had brought with her and ate it slowly, but by the time she had finished, the dwarf had still not appeared.

Sometimes she heard a noise and turned her head. But it was only a leaf falling from a branch of the oak tree and landing gently on the mossy ground.

She waited the whole morning, until in the distance she could hear the bell ringing for lunch.

She stood up, looked around her, and said: 'Dwarf, I'm very cross. I'm going to have my lunch now. But I will come back after lunch. I hope you will stick to your promise and reappear. If you don't, I will never again trust a living soul.'

And having said that, she went home.

IV

After lunch, Isabel put her basket over her arm and went into the kitchen to ask cook to give her some chocolate and raisins. As usual at that time of day, cook was in a grumpy mood. Isabel had to ask her several times, but finally she got what she wanted.

She put the chocolate and raisins in her basket and ran out to the garden.

When she reached the old oak tree she called out: 'Dwarf!'

But no one replied.

Once again she called: 'Dwarf, my dear friend dwarf, I'm here! It's me!'

But all around she could see only trees, moss, ferns, reeds and quivering grasses.

She painstakingly searched throughout the little wood. But the dwarf was so small he could hide anywhere. If he didn't wish to be seen, it would be impossible to find him. Besides, he might already be far away, in the park or in the pine forest.

Isabel was beginning to despair.

She sat down on the ground beside the pretty little house she had built and began to cry.

Then she raised her head and said out loud:

'Dwarf, you broke your promise. You're a liar and a coward.'

No sooner had she said this than she felt something hit her on the head. It was an acorn that someone had thrown rather hard. Looking up, she saw the dwarf sitting astride a branch. He was clearly furious.

His face was bright red and he was vigorously shaking his beard. Wagging one finger, he shouted: 'I won't have it! I won't have you calling me a liar and a coward. I am three hundred years old and no one has ever called me such names.'

'I'm sorry,' she said. 'I thought you weren't coming back.'

'I always keep my word,' the little man declared.

And leaping from branch to branch, he came down from the tree.

Isabel held out her two cupped hands, and the dwarf landed on them.

He really was a dwarf.

His suit was made of green cloth and his boots of brown leather. Around his waist he wore a wide belt with a silver dagger, and on his head was a green woollen hat the same colour as his suit, and decorated with a feather.

Very carefully and respectfully, Isabel put him

down on the ground.

She felt so happy to see him there before her, with his long white beard and his red face, that she began to clap her hands with joy, singing: 'I'm so happy, so happy, so happy!'

The dwarf chuckled and said: 'You don't need to make such a fuss.'

Isabel took the chocolate and raisins out of the basket, and the two of them sat on the ground eating the gifts of friendship.

From that day on, they became the best of friends.

At four o'clock every afternoon, when she came home from school, they would meet by the old oak tree.

He would perch on her shoulder and together they would roam through the garden. If someone appeared, Isabel would hide him in her pocket, or in the basket she always carried filled with flowers.

He taught her many things.

'How do you know so many things when you don't have any books and never went to school or university?' she asked him one day.

'Well,' he replied, 'we dwarves live for five hundred years and so we have time to see a lot, hear a lot and think a lot. And we have a good memory.

When we are young, the old dwarves tell us everything they have seen during the five centuries they have lived, and they also tell us everything that their parents taught them. And a dwarf only has to hear something once to remember it for ever more. That's why I can tell you stories about things that happened more than a thousand years ago. We also travel a lot.'

'How can you travel with such tiny legs?' asked Isabel.

'We travel the world on the backs of birds. We are great friends with the birds. When they migrate in flocks in spring and autumn, they take us with them whenever we want a change of scene or to go off and see the world. I've been to Persia, the North Pole and India, and I've flown with a white stork from Alsace to North Africa. That's why I know all the Earth's languages, both of men and of animals. I can speak to a Turk, and I can speak to a partridge.'

Isabel listened in amazement.

The dwarf told her stories about the past, about the Moors, and about warriors, sailors, princesses and kings of old. Then he talked about far-flung lands: he described the caravans of camels that slowly cross the vast Sahara Desert, and he described the Eskimos who live at the North Pole in houses made of ice.

But there was one thing the dwarf never told her about: his own life. She asked him in vain why he lived alone in their garden, far away from all the other dwarves.

'I cannot answer you now,' he would say. 'First I need to get to know you better, to see if you deserve to hear my story.'

That winter, when she had a lot of studying to do, Isabel would go to the garden, fill her basket with violets and camellias and bring the dwarf into the house, hidden among the flowers. For they had agreed she would tell no one that she knew a dwarf.

He would sit on top of the French dictionary on the school-room table and explain Isabel's lessons to her.

He was a very good explainer.

With his help Isabel quickly realised that history, science, geography and grammar were actually fun, but the dwarf's great speciality was mathematics. He could solve any problem and do sums in his head in a second.

Isabel would ask him: 'What is 563 times 432?'

And the dwarf would immediately reply: '243,216.'

And so a year passed. Winter, spring and summer went by, and autumn returned.

One afternoon, the dwarf said to Isabel: 'Tomorrow is Sunday and it will be one year since we met. Now I know that I can trust you. That's why tomorrow I will tell you my story. As soon as you have finished your lunch, come and meet me by the lake in the park.'

And so it was. The following day, at the appointed time and place, Isabel was there waiting.

The lake was in the middle of the park, in the most deserted part of the whole estate. The high branches of the planes, oaks and lime trees criss-crossed the sky. The light was green and golden, and the ground was covered in leaves. Here and there lay fallen twigs and branches. And from time to time, suddenly, a bird would call.

Isabel and the dwarf sat down on an old fallen tree trunk covered in moss.

The dwarf began to tell his story: 'A long time ago, everywhere around here was covered in dense forest, and it was a very wild, remote place. Today, there are only a handful of ancient oak and chestnut trees left, which you can still see here in this park. At that time, the forest stretched for many leagues and was completely inhabited by dwarves. There were very few people. In total, only ten woodmen and three friars lived hereabouts. The monastery was very small, with four cells, a refectory and a chapel. The fourth cell was for travellers who would sometimes come and ask the friars for shelter when evening fell. All that remains of the monastery now are those two ivy-covered walls over there. Everything else has gone. The monastery was already in ruins when the walls surrounding this estate were being built, so whenever the stonemasons needed more stone, they would come and take them from the monastery walls, which slowly disappeared, carried away bit by bit.

But back then, the monastery, although small and poor, was a lovely place, and when its bell rang for matins and the *Ave Maria,* it echoed the peacefulness of these woods.

The dwarves hid from the woodmen and the travellers who passed through the forest, but they were the best of friends with the monks. When the monastery was built ten centuries ago, it was they who helped the friars build the walls and carve the wooden pews. For dwarves are great carpenters and excellent stonemasons. They also taught the friars many of their secrets. They taught them how to speak to the birds, how to recognise medicinal plants, and how to build homes underground. Underneath the monastery chapel was a room with a secret entrance, built by the dwarves.

During the last hundred years, the city has grown a lot. Every year it advances further and now it almost touches the walls of this estate. In those days, though, the city was small and far away. Travellers passed by at a distance, along the road, and it was very rare for anyone to enter the forest. Sometimes hunters would appear. Then the whinnying of horses, the barking of hounds and the sounding of horns would invade the light and delicate air of the morning. Those were days of great disruption. Hares running around like mad, arrows whistling through the air, startled deer fleeing, and birds dizzily flapping, without a moment's rest. But as evening fell, the hunters would call off their hounds and leave. Peace would once again return to the forest. All you could hear were birds singing, the breeze whispering in the leaves, and the occasional twig snapping.

Then one day something terrible happened: attracted by the vastness of the impenetrable forest, some bandits came and set up camp. No one would have dared pursue them there. They built a secret hideout where they lived and kept all the things they had stolen. The bandits became the kings of the forest. The terrified woodmen fled with their families. All this happened during the autumn, and shortly afterwards, there was a great hunt. The sun had just risen, its slanting rays piercing the shade among the dark tree trunks, and the morning mist was still hanging in the air when we saw the hunters arrive. The horses neighed, the hounds bounded along and the men were cheerily laughing and talking, holding the reins with one hand and resting the other on their hip. They had heard there were bandits in the forest, but they weren't afraid of them, because they trusted in their weapons, their fierce hounds, their swift horses and in their own strength and courage.

But the bandits whistled with glee when, hidden in their lair, they saw the hunters come deeper into the forest.

"Let's hunt *them,*" they said to each other.

They quickly agreed a plan.

The horsemen hunted all morning, but didn't catch a single thing, because the bandits were always one step ahead of them, scaring away the animals.

"It looks like the bandits have hunted everything," said one of the horsemen, laughing.

"Maybe it would be better if we went no further," said another. "There are only seven of us and people say there are more than twenty of them."

"We are only seven," interrupted a third hunter, "but we have ten hounds, good horses and good guns. And as you can see, they aren't brave enough to show themselves to us."

And with these jokey comments, they carried on deeper into the forest.

The day was warming up and, when it was nearly midday, the horsemen made their way to a place where there was a small stream.

But the bandits were watching, and before the horsemen could dismount and the hounds begin drinking, the bandits chased a buck deer towards the hunters.

When they saw the animal, horsemen and hounds forgot all about their thirst and set off like lightning, chasing after their prey with shouts and yelps of joy.

The buck, however, was young, agile and strong, and the horsemen had to chase it for a long time before catching it.

This took them even further into the woods.

When they had killed the deer, they decided not to hunt any more that day and headed home.

On their way back they once again stopped beside the stream. The horsemen dismounted and everyone drank: first the men, then the horses and finally the hounds.

Perched in the trees, hidden by the dense foliage, the bandits were watching. When all ten hounds were gathered together drinking from the stream, the bandits opened fire on them.

Seven hounds fell immediately. The other three fled in terror and disappeared whimpering into the trees.

All was confusion. Two of the horses bolted. The others kicked and bucked and reared.

Then, at a given signal, the bandits all leaped down from the trees.

The battle was short-lived. In the blink of an eye the twenty bandits surrounded, defeated and disarmed the seven hunters. Then they seized their costly silver spurs, leather boots, fine riding jackets, feathered hats, and their horses. Barefoot, half-naked and wounded, and without their horses, the seven hunters made their miserable way home.

From that day on, there were no more hunts. Never again was the long blast of hunting horns and the happy hullabaloo of hounds heard beneath these trees. Never again did a hunter venture into the forest where the bandits now reigned.

V

All this happened more than two centuries ago, when I was still very young. I saw everything clearly with my own eyes, because I was right beside the stream, hidden inside the hollow trunk of an old chestnut tree. On a branch above me were perched two bandits, who said to each other: "We're the hunters of the hunters!"

From then on, this place was plunged into a deep peace. The trees grew into a silent leafy wilderness, ever thicker and darker, their branches multiplying. The ferns measured a yard high and the moss gradually covered all the stones. The woodmen had gone, the hunters had gone, the travellers had gone.

Only the three friars remained in their monastery.

They were so poor they had nothing to fear from the bandits. They had nothing worth stealing.

Shortly after arriving in the forest, the bandits' ringleader paid the friars a visit.

He glanced disdainfully at the four cells

containing only thin straw pallets and little crosses made from two sticks tied together.

He visited the refectory, where he saw only four stools, one table and a few bowls. Then he went to the chapel. He saw the rough-hewn wooden saints carved by one of the friars, and examined the altar they had made from cork. None of these things tempted him.

"Well," he said to the friars, "you can stay here, but on one condition. I've heard that you know a lot about medicine."

"We know how to make a tea from dried leaves that drives away fevers. We know how to make various types of poultices from herbs to heal wounds. And we know how to make a syrup to ease a cough."

"Very well. From now on, you will be our doctors. Given the lives we lead, we often get caught in a downpour when we stay out all night waiting to rob passing travellers. For this reason, we suffer terribly from colds and have a great need of teas and syrups. And we also need your poultices, because we're always getting into fights and our bodies are always covered in cuts and bruises. So we're going to make a deal with you: you will treat us when we're sick, and in return for this I will allow you to go on living here."

And so it was.

The years went by, and, with each year that passed, the bandits grew richer and richer.

At night they would take to the roads, hold up travellers and rob them of their coins, jewels, clothes and horses. No one could pursue them, because as soon as day broke, they would return to the forest where no one else dared follow.

Thus they built up a vast amount of treasure, which they kept in their cabins, in two large leather chests.

It was said they had killed more than a hundred people, and sometimes, at dawn, they returned from their robberies with their hands covered in blood.

The friars found these stories deeply distressing and decided to go and speak to the leader of the bandits.

"Brother," said the oldest friar, "the life you are leading is the life of a wild beast, not that of a man. Stealing is a terrible thing, but killing is far worse."

But the bandit roared with laughter and replied: "Those who are strong have the right to steal and to kill the weak. We are the strongest and so we have the right to do whatever we want."

"Brother," said the friar, "what you are saying is

neither just nor true."

"Friar," shouted the bandit, "I don't want to hear about truth or justice. If you speak more of such things, I will have your tongue cut out."

And with other such bloodcurdling threats and insults, the bandit sent the friars away.

But the years passed and the bandits grew old. They became unsteady on their feet, and their eyesight and aim began to fail them. In winter, when they got caught in the rain, they all came down with heavy colds. They coughed for months on end, and no tea or syrup could cure them.

VI

Then one day the wheel of fortune turned.

News spread that a very wealthy merchant was on his way from the city carrying jewellery, money and a large cargo of silks, rugs and velvets.

The bandits decided to rob him.

"I'm going to make myself some fine new suits of clothes," said one of them.

"I'm going to put some rugs down in my house," said another.

"I'm going to hang some curtains at my windows," said a third.

And in the stillness of the night, wrapped in

their cloaks, the twenty highwaymen hid by the side of the road.

There was no moon and the night was very dark indeed.

They waited for over an hour. It was very cold. The bandits crouched behind a bush, huddling together trying to keep warm. But an icy wind that cut through everything was blowing down from the plains, and soon they all began to cough and sneeze.

"All these nights out in the elements will be the death of me," grumbled one of them.

"I have a pain in my chest," grumbled another.

"I'm too old for this sort of thing," grumbled the third.

"It's high time we retired," grumbled a fourth.

"Who said anything about retiring?" thundered the leader.

But then a voice whispered: "Sssh! Sssh! Look!"

They all turned their heads to the left.

In the distance, on the dark highway, they could hear the far-off sound of horses and wagons.

They waited with bated breath.

The sound came closer, and in the pitch-black night they began to make out some slowly approaching figures.

One of the bandits who was posted further

to the left, crept over to his companions and told them: "There are four closed wagons and ten men on horseback."

"That's too many for us," whispered the voice that had said, "It's high time we retired."

"We should beat a hasty retreat," said another.

"Retreat? Never!" interrupted the ringleader. "They're loaded with gold, silver, jewels and silks. There are only ten horsemen. The merchant must be in one of the wagons, and the other three filled with merchandise. There are twenty of us valiant men. We'll finish them off in no time at all. Don't talk of retreating. We're stronger than them! If anyone talks any more about retreating, I'll knock his block off."

No one dared disagree.

But the ringleader's calculations were wrong.

For, knowing that these places were infested with highwaymen, the merchant had brought with him not only the ten men on horseback, but another ten armed men, hiding among the merchandise.

The wagons slowly drew closer.

It was getting colder and colder. There came the sound of eleven coughs and six sneezes.

"Silence," ordered the ringleader. "Everyone take up your positions, and make sure no one coughs."

With great difficulty, the bandits suppressed

their coughs.

The wagons approached. When they were ten yards away, the ringleader ordered: "Everyone onto the road!"

The twenty men instantly leaped out of the thicket and surrounded the wagons.

The horses stopped dead and the bandits, pointing their weapons at them, shouted: "Hands up!"

The ten men on horseback did as they were told, and the bandits approached the wagon.

At that moment, though, the merchant's ten armed men, hidden among the baggage, opened fire.

Ten bandits were wounded and the others, terrified by the unexpected response, ran away.

"We're done for!" one of them shouted.

And they all began to flee.

But the men on horseback raced after them, stopping them from reaching the woods.

Half an hour of turmoil and fighting ensured, and the bandits were utterly defeated. Almost all of them were seriously wounded, and all those who hadn't fled were disarmed and their hands bound with ropes.

Only one managed to escape: the ringleader.

In the midst of the fighting, he had fallen to the ground with a wound to his chest.

However, under cover of the surrounding darkness and disorder, he managed to crawl away from the road and hide in a thicket.

When the battle was over, the merchant told his men to put the wounded in the wagons, and the convoy continued its journey to the next city. The bandits who could walk followed on foot, tied together and surrounded by men on horseback.

When they were all far enough away, the ringleader emerged from the thicket and headed back into the forest.

Just inside the woods were the horses the bandits had left behind, tied to the trees, waiting for them.

The ringleader mounted his horse and managed to ride through the night towards the monastery, where he arrived at daybreak.

The three friars laid him in the cell set aside for travellers, and which had been left unused for so many years.

They examined him, washed his wound and dressed it with soothing herbs.

By the following day, however, the bandit's condition had worsened. He was burning up with fever and could scarcely open his eyes. He asked the oldest friar, who was called Brother João, to hear his confession.

For an hour, the bandit recounted his crimes. At the end, he said: "Brother, now you know my sins. You know how many people I have robbed and how many people I have killed, beaten and wounded. You know all the suffering I have caused in this world. Now I would like to wipe away the evil I have done. I would like to be able to go back and live my life another way. All the crimes I committed, I committed for the love of money. When I was a child, I was poor and ran barefoot in the streets. That was when I began to envy the wealthy. I envied their bags of gold, their velvet clothes, their jewels, their opulent houses. I decided I wanted to be rich. For more than twenty years I robbed and killed to make myself rich. There never seemed to be enough gold to satisfy me. The richer I became, the more I loved and wanted money. Out there in the middle of the forest, on the other side of the stream, under a big round stone between an oak and a birch tree, are buried two large chests filled with gold coins. That gold is the fruit of my crimes. Because of these coins, many people have suffered, wept and died. Friar, transform that evil fruit into something good. Do good works with this money. Give this money to a good person who will spend it on doing good, to wipe away the evil I have done. But take care, friar: the person to whom you give the money must have a soul that is completely pure, for money is a poison that destroys even the strongest spirits."

The friar promised the bandit he would do as he asked, and gave him absolution.

A few hours later, the bandit died.

The friars buried him, shedding many tears and filled with pity, but filled, too, with joy because they had seen with their own eyes that the sinner had died repentant.

VII

Three days later, after discussing the matter at length, the four friars summoned the dwarves and told them what had happened.

"We already know where the bandits' treasure is," said the King of the Dwarves. "But the chests are enormous and we would need a cart to transport them."

"How will we get a cart?" asked the youngest friar, who was called Brother António.

"We will make one," said the King of the Dwarves.

And for a week, we dwarves worked tirelessly

cutting down trees, planing the trunks and hammering in nails.

By the end of the week our work was done, and very good it was too. We hitched up the cart to the bandit's horse and went to dig up the chests.

They were extremely heavy and we had to transport them one at a time.

But when we reached the monastery, we encountered a problem: the chests were so big they didn't fit in any of the cells or even the refectory. And putting them in the chapel was unthinkable.

That's why we dwarves built an underground chamber beneath the chapel with its own secret entrance. That is where the chests were kept, and where they still are!'

'They're still there?' asked Isabel.

'Yes,' sighed the dwarf, 'and that's my big problem. I don't know what to do with them!'

'So the friars didn't give them to some very good man?'

'Alas!' exclaimed the dwarf. 'No very good man ever appeared.'

And he continued with his story: 'After that night when all the bandits were captured, there was great rejoicing in the city.

"We're free from the highwaymen," everyone

said. "Now we can walk the roads in peace and even go through the forest."

Sometime later, rumours began to spread that the bandits had left hidden treasure somewhere in the forest.

Things went from bad to worse. The forest was invaded by groups of adventurers looking for the stolen gold. They seemed almost crazy. They dug holes all over the place and sawed up the oldest and most beautiful of the trees to see if there was anything hidden inside the trunk. We dwarves had no place to hide.'

'Why didn't the friars give them the treasure, to make them go away?' asked Isabel.

'Because the invaders were very bad people. They spent the whole day fighting with each other and talking only about money. Fortunately, since they didn't find anything, after a while, they went away and left us in peace.

The years went by and the friars got older and older.

The forest began to be inhabited again. It filled up with woodmen, and travellers passed through here every day.

One day, however, a terrible epidemic spread throughout the whole region.

The three friars became sick.

After seven days of illness they sensed that the hour of their death was nigh.

We dwarves went to visit them, and seeing them so ill we all began to weep.

"Dear brother dwarves," said Brother João, "you shouldn't weep. We are very old and we desire the other world more than this one. Our spirits are lifted by the blessing of God, which may grant that we all die on the same day, for we would suffer terribly if we were separated. Only one thing troubles us: the bandits' treasure. Unfortunately, it was not possible to carry out the promise we made to their ringleader. For this reason, we are going to leave the gold in your hands. Seek, and seek well, for you will have to find someone to give it to."

The following day the three friars died, and the Angels came down to carry their souls up to heaven.

The monastery was now uninhabited and slowly began to fall into ruin.

We dwarves didn't know what we should do with all that heavy, cumbersome gold. The years went by, and we were unable to find any man who was entirely good.

Until one day a gentleman from the city purchased part of the forest, precisely the part where the old monastery was located and where we now are. He decided to build a country estate, right here. Men came and cut down almost all the trees: only this park remained as it was. After that, they began to cultivate the fields. Then, so that no one would steal his crops, flowers or fruit, the gentleman ordered that a high wall be built around the estate. That was when they took almost all the stones from the monastery, leaving only two walls.

Now, we dwarves love our liberty and cannot bear to feel imprisoned. Knowing that there was a wall around us took away all our happiness. For this reason, our king gathered together his council.

"This place," he said, "has become uninhabitable. We must travel to the forests of the North. Unfortunately, we have still not managed to find a home for the bandits' treasure. One of us will have to stay behind to look after the chests until he finds someone he can entrust them to."

We drew lots to decide who should stay, and I, alas, was the one who drew the short straw.

When autumn came, all my friends and companions mounted astride the wild ducks and flew off to the forests of the North.

That was more than two hundred years ago. And for all of that time I have lived here alone, far from my friends and relatives, imprisoned within the walls of this estate, tied to the bandits' treasure!'

'Oh, what a sad story!' sighed Isabel. 'We must find a solution.'

'Perhaps you can help me. I'm a dwarf and I don't speak to anyone. How am I to find the man I need?'

Isabel was silent, thinking.

After a few minutes, she exclaimed: 'I know!'

'Tell me, tell me!' exclaimed the dwarf.

'Give the treasure to my music teacher. He's an extraordinary man. His name is Cláudio and he's twenty-three years old. He spends the whole day playing the violin, and he also writes poetry. He's always saying: "Neither fortune, glory nor money count for a jot or a tittle. Only truth and beauty can give us happiness." He's a poet.'

'That seems a good idea to me,' said the dwarf. 'I've always liked poets.'

'Look,' said Isabel, 'tomorrow he's coming to give me a music lesson and I will bring him here.'

VIII

The following day, when Cláudio arrived, Isabel told him the story of the treasure.

He thought it was a very pretty story and wasn't in the least surprised.

'Now we'll go and meet the dwarf,' said Isabel.

And the two of them set off into the park.

The dwarf was already waiting for them beside the lake in the green and gold light filtering through the high leaves.

After introducing him to the music teacher, Isabel asked: 'Dwarf, do you want to show us the treasure?'

'Come with me,' said the little man.

And together they made their way through the park. From time to time a yellowing leaf detached itself from a branch, twirled twice in the air and fell to the ground, making only the faintest of sounds.

After ten minutes, they came to two very old stone walls, set at right angles and covered in moss and creepers.

'This is where the treasure is kept. These two walls are all that remain of the chapel. Now watch carefully,' said the dwarf.

And taking his dagger from his belt, he inserted the blade into a crack between two stones. The stones moved apart to reveal an opening and some steps.

'We dwarves made this,' said the dwarf proudly. 'See how skilful we are. Centuries later the mechanism still works. The chests are down there, so now we need to go down these steps.'

The little man began to jump from step to step.

'It's too dark. I can't go down there – I can't see a thing!' exclaimed Isabel.

'There are candles here,' shouted the dwarf.

'And I have matches,' said Cláudio.

He lit a match and took Isabel's hand. Together they went down the steps.

Inside the chamber, it smelled damp and musty.

The music teacher lit the candles in two candlesticks that had been left on a table.

The chests were enormous and made of leather hooped with iron. They were very, very old.

The teacher opened the chests. In the flickering light of the candles, the gold glittered and sparkled. There were piles and piles of coins, round and shining.

Isabel grabbed two handfuls and let the coins fall slowly through her fingers, tinkling against each other.

'It's beautiful,' she said.

The dwarf turned towards Cláudio.

'If you want, I'll give you all of this gold.'

But Cláudio shook his head and started whistling.

'So what are we to do?' asked the dwarf.

'I don't want it,' replied the musician. 'It's too much. It's too much money. If it's all right with you, I'll take just a few coins to buy a new violin.'

'That's impossible. Brother João promised the bandits' ringleader that he would give the gold to one person. All of it to one person. That's what was agreed, and I cannot break that promise. If I'd had instructions to distribute the coins, I would have done so long ago. Indulge me: take the gold and distribute it however you wish.'

'I can't. I would become a prisoner of the money just like you. I would be filled with doubts and problems. I would have to draw up endless accounts. It would all be very complicated indeed. Money is a poison when taken in large doses. I'm afraid your gold would poison my life.'

'So what can we do?' asked Isabel disconsolately.

'Oh dear,' sighed the dwarf. 'I can't see me ever being free of these two chests!'

The three of them stood there in silence, thinking.

Suddenly, the music teacher exclaimed: 'I have an idea. I know what we should do with the treasure.'

'Tell us, please,' begged the dwarf.

'I have a friend called Doctor Máximo who is very old and very wise. From a very young age he has dedicated his whole life to a single dream: discovering how to turn stones into gold. He thinks of nothing else. Once he was very rich, but now he's ruined, because he has spent his entire fortune on laboratories and experiments. People in the city make fun of him and say he's crazy. He wanders the streets talking to himself, even arguing with himself. Boys throw stones at him and shout: "Turn those into gold."

He never gets angry, for he's a very good man, and I've never seen him wish anyone ill.'

'But why would a good man think so much about gold?' asked the dwarf.

'Well, it's not because he wants to be rich. It's for the sake of science. Furthermore, he says that once he's able to turn stones into gold, he will use it to make all the poor folk wealthy. A few days ago, he took me to his laboratory, showed me a tank filled with stones and told me: "I'm now performing my final experiment. If this experiment fails, I will never be able to do another, because I've spent all I have setting up this one. I've carried out so many experiments in my life, and all of them have failed.

But this one must work. I've poured all my learning into it, the fruit of sixty years of study!"

He then began to pour into the tank bottle after bottle of green, purple and black liquids. He spent an hour doing this until all the stones were covered with a thick, dark liquid.

Then he closed the shutters, turned to me and said: "Let's go."

We went out and locked the door. He then explained to me: "The stones need to remain for a month in the dark, immersed in that combination of liquids, which they will slowly absorb. Today is the 20th of October. By the 20th of November, the stones should have been transformed into gold. If this experiment fails, it will be because my life has failed. But if this experiment works, I will be a completely happy man. And I will make many other people happy. Three days from now, the stones should all be black. Three days later, they should all be blue. Three days after that, they should be white. Then, after the tenth day, the stones should start turning yellow, until they all turn to gold! For the next month I will be so consumed with impatience that I have to get away from here. I will go to the countryside. There I can rest and try to distract myself. But I need to ask you a favour: while I am gone, please look after the key of the laboratory for me. If I don't have the key, it will be easier for me to resist the temptation to come back and hang around the laboratory. Besides, I'm very absent-minded, my brain is tired and I never know where I've put things. I'm afraid of losing the key while I'm away."

And with those words Doctor Máximo handed me the key, and I have been carrying it in my pocket ever since.

An hour later, the Doctor left for the countryside. After three days, I could resist no longer. I went to the laboratory. The stones had not turned black, but were just the same as before. After three more days, I went back to the laboratory. The stones had not turned blue; they were still the same as before. Once again, after three more days, I returned to the laboratory: the stones had still not changed.

Today is the tenth day. This morning I went to see the stones. They are exactly the same as before.'

'So the experiment has failed!' exclaimed Isabel.

'Yes,' said Cláudio. 'But there is a solution: we could take out the stones and put all this gold into the tank in the laboratory. That way, Doctor Máximo will think his experiment has worked. And so this gold, which was the cause of so many crimes and so much suffering, will be transformed into joy.'

'That's a wonderful idea,' said Isabel, 'but won't Doctor Máximo be surprised when he sees that the stones have turned not only into gold, but also into coins?'

'Ah, yes, that's very true,' replied the young man. 'But what else can we do?'

'That's not a problem,' said the dwarf. 'We dwarves are very skilled in the art of melting down metal. In less than three days I can melt down the coins and shape them into stones. Just leave it to me and I'll get straight to work. Come back and meet me beside the lake in three days' time.'

'While you're working on the gold, I'll get rid of the stones that are in the laboratory tank,' said the music teacher.

And giving Isabel his hand, they clambered back out of the underground chamber.

IX

Many centuries earlier, the dwarves had excavated their subterranean palace beneath Isabel's family estate.

That was where the dwarf went to get the tools he needed, and within three days, as promised, he had melted down the gold and cast it into the shapes of stones. Then the music teacher came with a suitcase to fetch the treasure. But there were so many golden stones that they needed to make many trips. Indeed, it took them more than two weeks, but, by 19th November, everything was ready. On the morning of 20th November, the young music teacher knocked on the door of old Doctor Máximo, who had returned from the countryside the previous day.

'I've brought you the key,' he said.

'Thank you,' replied the alchemist. 'But don't leave me now. Come with me to the laboratory. I'm not brave enough to be alone at such an important moment.'

'Cheer up, my friend. You have worked and studied so hard that your experiment is sure to have succeeded.'

'Ah,' sighed the old man, 'my hopes are shattered. There have been so many failed experiments! My calculations are correct, I know they are correct, but when I run the experiments something always goes wrong. If I have failed this time I will never again have the courage to do anything.'

As they entered the laboratory, Doctor Máximo's hands were trembling.

'Will you open the shutters?' he asked his friend. The light filled the large room packed with machines, alembics, retorts and flasks.

Using a pair of pincers, the music teacher lifted a stone out of the tank and held it up in the air.

'Gold!' cried the alchemist.

He grabbed the metal stone and turned it round and round. Then he began to laugh and cry at the same time.

'I can hardly believe what I'm seeing!' he said. 'I'm not a silly old failure any more. I have proved my theories to be right. The experiment didn't fail. I am so happy, so very happy! And I am going to make everyone around me happy too!'

By the next day, news of the great discovery had already spread throughout the city. The newspapers spoke of nothing else. Curious onlookers surrounded the laboratory. That night there were fireworks.

The president of the academy of sciences, the chancellor of the university and the chairman of the municipal council came in person to visit Doctor Máximo and gave the following speech:

'Doctor, you are one of the wise men of the universe. Your discovery honours our city and we are very proud of you. The academy of sciences, the university and the municipal council all congratulate you on your achievement. Your discovery is a remarkable event, indeed one of the greatest events in this century of progress. We have already decreed that you should be awarded the highest rank of the Order of Public Merit. And we have also decreed that next Thursday there will be a public holiday in your honour. And on the same day, to celebrate your great discovery, a magnificent ceremony will take place in the square outside the city hall, again in your honour, and during that ceremony we will have the great honour of presenting you with the decoration that has been bestowed upon you.'

'Thank you, thank you so very much,' said Doctor Máximo. 'That will be perfect, because, at the end of the ceremony, I will use the occasion to distribute my gold stones to the poor of the city.'

The president of the academy, the chancellor of the university and the chairman of the municipal council looked at each other and left, muttering: 'That's all very noble and original, but very strange too!'

Moments later, there was another knock on Doctor Máximo's door.

Outside stood a queue of bankers and merchants.

The alchemist received them one by one.

'Dear friend,' said the first, 'gold is a precious metal. It is the food, the blood and the very essence of civilisation. It must be used well. I have come to teach you how to use your gold. I have brought you a tremendous business proposition, which will benefit us both enormously.'

'I am very grateful,' replied the doctor, 'but I am an alchemist, not a businessman. I made my discovery out of love of science, not money. Next Thursday, I will distribute all my gold to the poor of the city. And later, when I carry out more experiments, I will spread the gold even further among the poor of other cities. Thus, slowly but surely, I will begin to remedy the inequalities of this world.'

Crimson with shock and confusion, the businessman interrupted him: 'But I am offering you an extraordinary business opportunity! One that will guarantee a return of fifty per cent a year!'

'But I don't love money, and I can change stones into gold. Why would I want to earn still more?'

The businessman left, still angry and confused.

One by one, the other businessmen filed into the inventor's study.

They all proposed business schemes and all received the same response.

They left angrily, mumbling: 'The fellow's a dangerous madman.'

The following morning, the alchemist was working in his laboratory.

He was wearing white overalls, and, with his glasses perched on the tip of his nose, he was peering attentively at a retort filled with a thick green, gloopy liquid.

The doorbell rang and he interrupted his observations to go and open the door, only to find some of the same businessmen who had come to see him the day before. This time there were only seven of them, but these were the seven richest men in the city.

'I hope you haven't come to talk to me about business!' exclaimed the alchemist.

'Not at all, dear friend,' said the most important of the men, who went by the name of Mr Know-All. 'Today I have come to talk to you about science. I want you to show us round your laboratory and explain to us your studies and your discovery.'

Doctor Máximo looked at him in astonishment. He was a squat, ugly man, with bulging cheeks like a frog, which wobbled about on either side of his face. Everyone in the city knew he had no interest in science, only money.

But the wise old man was a friendly sort and immediately began showing them his retorts and other contraptions.

After an hour of explanations, the inventor told them: 'But the secrets of my science lie in here.'

And with these words he opened a door, and they went into a room where the walls were lined with books and the tables and chairs piled high with papers. On the back wall hung a blackboard covered with formulae scribbled in chalk.

'This,' continued Doctor Máximo, indicating the room around him, 'this is my study. Here is where I do my calculations and dream up the inventions that I later try out in the laboratory. On these papers are written the formulae of my discoveries, and all of my knowledge lies in these formulae. For I am old and I forget things, but everything is kept safe here in these papers.'

The seven businessmen looked at each other in silence, and then Mr Know-All said: 'Your discovery is a glory for science. In the field of culture, too, it is a notable occurrence. But in practical terms, in everyday life, your discovery is both a mistake and a disaster.'

'Why?' asked the wise old man.

'Your discovery will upset the established order. Until now, poor people have always worked to earn their living and rich people have worked to get richer. But from now on, no one will want to work any more.'

'No, no,' interrupted Doctor Máximo. 'People can't eat gold or clothe themselves in gold; they will still have to till the soil and make their clothes just as before.'

'Things will never again be as they were before!' growled one of the other businessmen. 'Gold was valuable because it was rare. If gold were abundant it would be worth very little. And then what would become of all those who have spent their lives scrimping and saving in order to lovingly stash a few gold coins at the back of a drawer? We will all be ruined!'

'I'm sorry, I'm sorry!' sighed the wise old man.

'This is unfair competition!' shouted a third businessman. 'It has taken us many years to build up our fortunes, but, in just one month, you have turned a pile of stones into treasure.'

'It simply can't go on,' said Mr Know-All. 'We greatly admire your talent, dear friend, but your experiments must not be repeated. We have come here today to speak to you in the utmost seriousness.

This cannot continue: you must assure us that you will stop your experiments.'

'A man of science,' replied the alchemist, 'cannot stop his work.'

'But we are asking you to stop,' said Mr Know-All.

'No!'

'Very well then. We are rich and powerful men and have many rich and powerful friends. From now on, we are your enemies and will find a way to put an end to your work.'

And the seven businessmen left, slamming the door behind them.

For the rest of the day and the next, Doctor Máximo could find not a moment's peace.

People knocked incessantly at his door. They came to make business proposals, or ask for loans, or suggest ideas and projects. Many of them asked the inventor to stop turning stones into gold.

The alchemist sighed, his head spinning.

'What shall I do?'

X

Finally, Thursday came.

The city was in a festive mood. Banners hung

from the windows and, down by the river, fire-crackers were being let off.

The entire population was crammed into the square outside the city hall, spilling over into the surrounding streets. The municipal band was playing celebratory music, and street hawkers were selling fizzy drinks and stones.

'Buy these stones, and the alchemist will turn them into gold!' they cried.

Flanked by the great and the good, the alchemist mounted a platform. Beside him was the music teacher, who was carrying the dwarf hidden in his pocket. Both of them were greatly amused by the goings-on, although the municipal band's rather off-key playing did occasionally set their teeth on edge.

Then the music came to an end, and the chairman of the municipal council, the president of the academy of sciences and the chancellor of the university each made a speech. The chancellor, who was the last to speak, finished by saying: 'Doctor Máximo deserves our maximum gratitude.'

There was loud applause, and the band played enthusiastically, while the chairman of the municipal council pinned the large medal of the Order of Public Merit on the wise inventor's lapel.

Then began the distribution of gold.

Four large chests had been placed on the platform.

Doctor Máximo lifted the lids and the dwarves' treasure glittered in the sunlight.

The guards cleared a path through the middle of the crowd and the poor began to line up. There were men, women, old people and children. They came barefoot and dressed in rags, their eyes shining in their pale, pinched faces as they looked up patiently and expectantly. It was impossible to believe that in so rich and beautiful a city there could be so many lives filled with misery. There were so many of them that they queued until sunset.

Stone by stone, Doctor Máximo distributed the treasure with his own hands. Indeed, as it happened, the number of gold stones was exactly equal to the number of poor.

The sun disappeared over the horizon out towards the sea and the sky turned deep red, silhouetting the houses all around.

The city filled with music and dancing. People strolled merrily through the streets, where coloured paper lanterns bobbed about in the breeze. People strummed their guitars on balconies, or danced in the squares.

Then there were fireworks. Great blossoms of

light burst in the sky, then dissolved into stars and fell slowly - purple, green, gold and blue - over the dark waters of the river.

The world seemed to have turned into one enormous party.

But Doctor Máximo could not share in this happiness. Once again flanked by the great and the good, he was hauled off to a banquet.

The alchemist was extremely tired, and the banquet seemed to him interminable. They were served three dishes of fish and four of roast meat. Then the puddings and sorbets appeared. To round it all off, there were toasts, tributes and yet more speeches.

Cláudio, who had also been invited (the alchemist had introduced him as his colleague), sat at the end of one of the tables with the dwarf in his pocket, and smiled as he watched the proceedings.

From time to time, he whispered softly, explaining to the dwarf the things he couldn't see, and surreptitiously feeding him little titbits.

'What an odd fellow,' commented a man sitting near him. 'He keeps talking to himself and putting food in his pocket.'

'He must be a very wise man,' replied another. 'Wise men are very odd creatures indeed.'

'Odd - and dangerous,' observed the first man.

'This discovery of man-made gold will only lead to trouble.'

'I agree: they say that gold will lose its value.'

And they looked worried and shook their heads.

When the banquet was over, Doctor Máximo was taken to a room by a group of very important men, who sat him down and talked at him for two hours without stopping.

It was after midnight before the alchemist was able to break free.

Then, after saying goodnight to the assembled guests, he went and found the music teacher and the two of them left. Outside, the city continued to celebrate: the streets were still full of people coming and going, laughing, singing and dancing under the coloured lanterns. The fireworks sent their greenish glow high into the sky, and tears of light fell slowly over the rooftops.

A woman passed by, shouting: 'Quick! There's a special display of fireworks down by the river!'

From a hill overlooking the city, a large lantern rose slowly into the night air and, somewhat unsteadily, set off on its dreamlike journey.

'This is a tremendous party. Look how happy everyone is. And it's all in your honour. Are you happy?' said Cláudio.

'I am happy, but I'm sad too!' said the alchemist. 'What will become of me? A little while ago those very important men told me that my experiments will be banned, because they're disrupting the city's business affairs. A friend of mine has warned me that I'm running great risks. It seems that there is a secret organisation among the merchants of this country, and they always band together against anyone who upsets their business interests. It's all very murky, for these people move in the shadows and are very powerful. What will become of me? My friend tells me that there are nine of them united against me. What shall I do?'

'There's only one piece of advice I can give you, my friend: call off your experiments and announce that you will never again turn stones into gold.'

'I can't do that. A scientist cannot abandon his work. It would be deeply shameful were I to turn my back on science after such a triumph.'

'Well,' sighed Cláudio, 'then we will have to find another solution. But it is late now. Let's think about it tomorrow.'

By now they had reached the door of Doctor Máximo's house. The two friends bade each other goodnight and the music teacher set off home.

The street, a little outside the city centre, was empty, for the crowds were still gathered in the streets and squares downtown, and along the quaysides overlooking the river.

The dwarf poked his head out of Cláudio's pocket and asked: 'Why do you want him to stop his experiments? He didn't discover anything at all. What difference would it make if he repeats them, since the experiments cannot succeed?'

'I want him to stop for two reasons. First, because if he repeats the experiment the stones will still be stones and he'll be terribly disappointed. Second, because if he continues with his experiments, he will never have any peace. The important men of the city will never leave him alone, and will come up with a thousand ways of persecuting and tormenting him.'

'So what should we do?'

'I don't know. I'm very worried. The bandits' gold has brought nothing but trouble.'

'It was won by very foul means,' commented the dwarf.

'But a solution will surely appear,' said the music teacher.

XI

That night, the dwarf slept at the young musician's house.

They were woken in the middle of the night by a loud ringing of bells.

'It's the firemen,' said Cláudio. 'A lantern must have fallen and set fire to something, but the firemen are already on their way to put it out.'

And both of them went back to sleep.

But in the morning, when they went out into the street, the city looked very messy and muddled. The ground was covered in dirty bits of papers, and extinguished lanterns hung limply from many balconies.

Throngs of people were gathered in the streets and squares, talking earnestly. The shop assistants stood in their doorways, watching. The cooks gathered in huddles at the corners of the square. Everyone was talking about the big news: during the night, Doctor Máximo's library and laboratory had burned down.

'It was a lantern that started the fire,' said an old man.

'Or some sort of explosion. There are always dangerous, highly explosive things in laboratories,' said a well-dressed gentleman.

'Nonsense!' cried a woman. 'The alchemist had acquired a lot of enemies. The powerful men here in the city said that his discovery would ruin them.

It was arson. It was Doctor Máximo's enemies who did this.'

Cláudio stepped away from the group and said to the dwarf: 'You see? A solution appeared. Let's go and find our friend.'

A police cordon had surrounded the laboratory, stopping curious onlookers from entering.

The firemen had already left, as the fire had been completely extinguished more than two hours earlier.

The music teacher explained that they were friends of the doctor, and the policemen let them through.

Doctor Máximo was all alone, surrounded by ashes and ruins. Of his library, there remained not a single book, manuscript or piece of paper. In the laboratory, all the flasks, test tubes and retorts had exploded. The floor was covered in water, broken glass, bits of burnt rubber, charred wood and twisted metal.

When he saw Cláudio, the alchemist opened his arms and exclaimed: 'Don't be distressed, my friend! This fire was my salvation! I feel happy and relieved. You see, a solution appeared. Without the manuscripts where I wrote down all my formulae and calculations, I cannot continue the experiments.

Just as well! My triumph had brought me many worries. This way, I still have my triumph but I'm free from my troubles. Now they will leave me in peace. I made a great scientific discovery, and no one can doubt my wisdom, but I have none of the complications that my discovery brought with it. My plan to turn stones into gold would have created enormous problems and brought me many enemies. But this fire has put an end to my problems. My enemies will lose interest in me, and I will devote myself to other projects.'

'In any case,' said the music teacher, 'you are the most famous man in the city! No one now would dare to make fun of you.'

'That is very true,' replied the alchemist. 'But I am tired of fame. Fame is a tiresome, complicated thing. All I want is a bit of peace.'

That same day, as evening fell, Isabel, the dwarf and Cláudio all sat down on a moss-covered bench at the far end of the park. They sat perfectly still, and silently watched the leaves falling slowly from the high branches above.

It was the dwarf who broke the silence.

'For three centuries I've lived here in the place where I was born,' he said, 'but today, the time has come for me to leave. I will miss this place very much, but I must go now and rejoin my brother dwarves in the forests of the North. Thank you, Isabel, and thank you, my dear musician. Thanks to you, Isabel, and you, Cláudio, and Doctor Máximo, I am finally free from the bandits' terrible treasure. The King of the Dwarves always told me: "Trust in children, wise men and artists."'

'Oh dear,' sighed Isabel. 'I will miss you so much, my dear dwarf. How will I ever get over you leaving?'

'When you are grown up,' said the music teacher, 'write down this story. Things that happen stay alive forever when they are written down.'

Nevertheless, despite Cláudio's kind advice, Isabel began to cry.

But then the dwarf made such a sensible speech that, after only a few minutes, she had wiped away her tears. Then a beautiful black bird with a yellow beak flew down from the top of an oak tree. Its feathers gleamed and its wings were broad and strong.

'What a beautiful bird!' exclaimed Isabel.

'This is the bird who will take me to the forests of the North, where my people are waiting for me. It is far, far away and we will fly for many long days.

We have to cross Spain, France, Alsace and then the sea. The time has come for us to say goodbye.'

The little man then bowed, kissed Isabel's hand, shook Cláudio's finger and jumped up onto the bird's back.

'Farewell, farewell,' he said. 'We will never forget each other.'

'Never,' replied Isabel. 'Never.'

The bird flapped its wings and rose into the air. The dwarf waved goodbye. His long white beard fluttered around his tiny little face, which looked both grave and cheerful, and as red as a strawberry.

The music teacher and Isabel followed the two travellers with their gaze far into the distance: they watched them soar over the fields and woods as they turned and headed North. Until, finally, they were no more than a tiny black dot. Then the two friends, arm in arm, walked slowly back to the house.

The park was empty and deserted. The tall canopies of the trees formed a green vault above them. The white patches on the trunks of the plane and birch trees stood out against the green. Not a single human voice or footstep could be heard. The leaves fell, twirling slowly in wide circles, and landed almost without a sound on the soft ground. Here and there, a twig snapped. Here and there, a bird sang. Quivering grasses danced in the faintest of breezes. The scent of autumn apples hung in the air.

The clear waters of the stream sang as they tumbled from stone to stone. It was the same stream that had refreshed those reckless hunters, those terrifying bandits and those wise dwarves, so grave and yet so cheerful.

Author's Note

The Tree and *The Mirror, or the Living Portrait* were inspired by two traditional Japanese stories.

Nevertheless, as the saying goes, 'every teller of a tale adds his own twist'.

When I was a child, a relative of mine sent me a series of books from a collection entitled *Tales from Old Japan*. Everything about these books fascinated me, from the stories and illustrations, down to the paper of the pages and the stamps on the wrapping paper they arrived in. It was my first encounter with the Orient. Each book told just one story, and one of those stories appears here as *The Mirror, or the Living Portrait*. But with the passage of time, I lost the books and forgot the names (which were unfamiliar to me) of the characters. So I wrote the story based on my recollections, sometimes vague, sometimes precise.

The Tree was told to me by the writer Isao Tesuka. To his story I added various new elements, variations and digressions. Thus, the poem about the paper lion is my translation of a traditional Japanese poem that I read, in English, in a book about Japan. The second poem, which appears at the end of the story, is my own.

The Tree

Once upon a time, long, long ago, far away on the archipelago of Japan, there was a tiny island on which grew an enormous tree.

The Japanese have a great love and respect for nature, and treat all trees, flowers, bushes and mosses with the utmost care and tenderness.

So the people of that island felt very happy and proud to possess such a big and beautiful tree. None of the other islands of Japan, not even the larger ones, had a tree as big as theirs. Even travellers passing through said they had never seen such a tall tree, not even in Korea or China, nor one with such a shapely, leafy crown.

On summer afternoons, people would come and sit beneath its spreading branches and admire its vast, rugged trunk. They would marvel at the sweet coolness of its shade, and the whispering of the breeze in its scented leaves.

And so it was for many generations.

But as time went on, a terrible problem arose, and no matter how much the islanders pondered and discussed it, no one could come up with a solution.

For, over the years, the tree had grown so tall, its branches so long, its foliage so thick and its crown so broad that, throughout the day, half the island lay permanently in shade, which meant that half the houses, streets, vegetable plots and gardens received no sun at all.

And in the shady half, the houses were growing damp, the streets gloomy, and the vegetable plots had no vegetables and the gardens no flowers. And the people who lived there were always pale and plagued with colds.

As the shade from the tree spread, so did the trouble it caused.

"What are we to do?" the people wailed. "What are we to do?"

***

Eventually they decided that all the islanders should gather together in a great council to examine the problem thoroughly and decide what they should do.

They talked for many days, and once everyone had had their say, they came to the sad conclusion that the tree must be cut down.

There were tears and sighs and lamentations.

The tree was old, beautiful and venerated by all. Doing away with it not only saddened the island's inhabitants, it frightened them too.

But there was no other solution, and in the end almost everyone agreed that the tree must be felled.

In its place, they would plant a small grove of cherry trees, since cherry trees never grow very tall.

***

Felling the tree was hard work, and everyone had to lend a hand.

Even when it had been cut down, however, the tree took up so much space that there was hardly any room left on the island for anything else. So the islanders started chopping it into pieces.

First, they cut off the boughs and branches and shared out the wood, so that each person could make something that would remind them of their beloved tree.

Some made little tables or verandahs for their houses, others made the frames for folding screens, while others made boxes, trays, bowls, spoons, combs and ladies' hairpins.

In the end, all that remained was the vast bare trunk that lay across the island from one end to the other.

Then sailors and shipbuilders began to arrive on the island, asking if they could use the tree's excellent timber to make boats.

But the islanders didn't want that. Once again, they gathered together in council and decreed: 'The inhabitants of this island do not wish to part with their tree, which before it grew too big, gave them such happiness and joy. Instead, we will build our own boat.'

And so it was. After the autumn rains, they left the trunk to dry for several long months. Then, once they were sure the timber was dry enough, they set to work.

The Japanese are a very intelligent people who work swiftly and meticulously. They are also excellent carpenters. So they quickly built a large and beautiful boat, all finely carved and painted in many colours.

Then they held a big party and the boat was launched.

That night there were fireworks, and all the streets and squares on the island were filled with blue, yellow and red paper lanterns.

***

From then on, the islanders' lives became far more exciting and varied, and almost all of them became richer.

Previously, because the island itself was so small, its inhabitants only had small fishing boats and could only sail as far as the neighbouring islands. Whenever someone needed to go further, they had to find a berth on one of the larger boats that called in from time to time.

Now everything changed. Thanks to the new boat, they could sail from island to island whenever they wanted, and go on long and very successful trading voyages.

Sometimes, on calm summer or autumn nights, groups of islanders would take the boat out onto the open sea to watch the full moon rise over the water.

Or they would sail round the island, hugging the

coast until they reached the island's southernmost tip, where they could admire the dark outline of the cliffs silhouetted against the shimmering blue of the moonlight.

Then, during the winter, they would talk about these excursions, comparing everything they had seen and discussing which had been the most beautiful night and which the most beautiful view.

***

Meanwhile, as time passed, the cherry trees they had planted continued to grow, becoming ever lovelier.

Because of this, the islanders began to hold an annual cherry blossom festival.

As winter drew to a close and the first signs of spring appeared, everyone's spirits rose.

The stonemasons, barrelmakers and carpenters came out to work in the open air, laughing and singing as they carved, hammered and sawed.

There was a great bustle of people hurrying through the streets, all rushing to the fabric shops to buy spring kimonos in readiness for the day when they could go out and gaze at the first flowers of spring.

And in the streets, gardens and fields, the quince trees, apple trees and cherry trees were already laden with tightly furled buds.

In the middle of the village the tame monkey appeared in its little blue coat and accompanied by his owner. The children and adults gathered round to admire the canny creature's skills.

The children were astonished when a big paper lion came swinging and swaying out into the street, flanked by two men wearing yellow kimonos. They went round all the streets and came to a halt beneath the branches of the cherry trees.

Then the men in yellow kimonos began to beat their drums, and the lion began to dance. One of the men started singing:

See the lion dance
Underneath the cherry trees
Swaying to the beat
Of the beating beating drum,
He'll make the blossoms open.

And the very next day, on every branch of every cherry tree, the little pink buds had all opened.

***

So, for many years, life on the island went on very happily and cheerfully, but despite all this happiness, and despite the flourishing trade and long voyages, everyone still thought wistfully of the old tree.

'How tall and beautiful it was!' they said.

'And how scented its shade!'

'How delicate and light the murmuring of the breeze among its leaves!'

'How rounded and shapely its crown!'

'How green and elegant its leaves!'

'How sweet the coolness beneath its branches on summer mornings!'

And so, in both thought and word, the tree was never forgotten.

***

The years went by.

Until the sailors and shipwrights made a terrible discovery: the wooden keel was beginning to rot.

'Heavens preserve us!' cried the islanders. 'We won't be able to go out to sea on moonlit nights or visit the other islands or keep on trading.'

But the traders reassured them.

'Thanks to our great big boat,' they said, 'we've been sailing from island to island for years now, buying and selling from port to port and with such success that we've made a lot of money. We have no other big trees on our island, and the trees we have would be sorely missed were we to cut them down, but now we can afford to go to the other islands and buy strong, sturdy timber from them. Then together we can build another big boat.'

Everyone applauded and quickly agreed to the plan. A few months later, the new boat was ready to be launched.

Then they hauled the old boat up onto the beach, and the islanders stood around, sad and silent, while the carpenters and caulkers examined it plank by plank.

The timber from the hull, deck and benches was almost all half-rotten and good only for firewood. But the main mast, which had been cut from the core of the old tree, was still sound and well-preserved.

'We ought to make something out of this mast that will remind us of our boat and our old tree,' said the island's chief.

After much thought, they decided to make a *biwa*, which is a kind of Japanese guitar.

When it was ready, all the islanders gathered

in the main square and sat in a circle around the island's finest musician, to hear the sound of the *biwa*.

However, as soon as the musician's fingers plucked the *biwa's* strings, from deep within the instrument came a voice, which sang:

The ancient tree
That sang in the breeze
Is now itself a song.

Then they all understood that the memory of the tree would never be lost, and would never cease to protect them, because poems pass from generation to generation and are always true to their people.

The Mirror, or the Living Portrait

A long, long time ago, there lived in a village in Japan a husband and wife who loved each other deeply and were deeply happy.

They had a very pretty little daughter, who was the very image of her mother, with the same dark, almond-shaped eyes, the same pale, transparent skin, the same small, round nose, and the same straight, black, thick, lustrous hair.

The three of them lived in a house that was very clean and pretty. The floor was covered with straw mats, and the rooms were divided by sliding screens made of paper. There was a wooden verandah on the southern and western sides of the house, and the house itself was surrounded by a wonderful garden full of mossy boulders and stone lanterns and planted with pine trees, bamboo, cherry trees, apple trees, azaleas, camellias, lilies and chrysanthemums. A little stream ran through the garden, tumbling from stone to stone and crossed by a wooden bridge. A wisteria twined about one of the verandah pillars, and, in spring, it hung heavy with long, mauve clusters of flowers that made the air dizzy with its scent. And the man and the woman wanted nothing more in the world than to live there with their daughter, the three of them together, in the peace of that house and the beauty of its garden.

But one day, the father, who was a tea merchant, had to travel to Kyoto, the capital of Japan, to deal with some business matters.

His wife was very worried, because in those days, journeys were slow, difficult and dangerous. She was afraid her husband would be attacked by highwaymen, or that he would fall ill alone in some unknown land, or would become lost, because Kyoto was very far away.

Her husband reassured her, explaining that he would not be travelling on his own, but in the company of other traders from the surrounding area. He told her he would be gone for as short a time as possible, and promised to bring back many wonderful presents from Kyoto.

So a few days later, he said goodbye to his wife and daughter, and left early the next morning.

***

He was gone for four months.

His wife counted off the days and weeks one by one. But already the petals of the cherry blossom had fallen, the clusters of wisteria had wilted, summer had passed, and the autumn moon shone down on the far-off mountains. Already, flocks of wild duck had begun crossing the darkening grey sky.

Then one day, in the late afternoon, as the wife was lighting the lamps, a neighbour knocked at the door and announced: 'I was up in the mountains and saw your husband in the distance.'

The woman quickly let down her long lustrous hair and carefully combed and pinned it up into a sleek, elaborate chignon. Then she put on her finest silk kimono, called her daughter and dressed her in her best clothes too, combing her dark fringe over her forehead. And while they were doing this, they laughed and clapped their hands with joy.

By the time the man reached the door of the

house, his wife and daughter were ready waiting for him, and both bowed low in greeting.

***

All three were overjoyed to be reunited.

The man gave his wife and daughter the presents he had brought: bolts of silk and cotton, fans and carved hairpins for his wife, and toys and dolls for his daughter.

Later, the three of them ate supper, sitting on a mat around a small, low table, laughing and talking in the soft glow of the paper lantern.

When they had finished eating, the daughter went to bed, and her mother and father were alone.

'I brought you another present,' said the husband. 'It's a surprise.'

'What is it?' asked his wife, full of curiosity.

'It's something unknown here, but in Kyoto and other large cities every woman has one. It's called a mirror.'

And the man opened a lacquer box and gave his wife a sheet of glass in a wooden frame.

The woman was speechless with surprise, gazing at the mirror.

'Tell me what you see,' asked her husband.

And she answered: 'I see the most beautiful young woman I've ever seen in my whole life. And strange though it may seem, she's wearing a blue kimono exactly like mine.'

'No, you silly goose,' said her husband smiling. 'What you see is yourself, because, like the water in the lake, the mirror reflects what it sees, only more exactly. That smiling woman is you!'

'Ah!' exclaimed the woman. 'It's like a living portrait!'

She was so amazed by the mirror that, for many days, she could think of nothing else. Whenever she was alone, she would open the lacquer box, take out the mirror and, kneeling on the mat, gaze at her own image. She never wearied of admiring her almond-shaped eyes, her oval face, her coral-pink lips and her thick, dark, lustrous hair.

Until one day, she realised she was becoming full of pride because of her beauty. She was becoming foolish, shallow and vain.

Troubled by this thought, she quickly put the mirror back in its box, stowed it away in a safe place and never again looked at herself.

***

Slowly the years passed, and the man, woman and child lived together happily in the peace of the house and the beauty of the garden.

As the daughter grew up, she came to look more and more like her mother, but she had only just turned fifteen when her mother fell ill. Doctors, priests and exorcists all came to the house, but none could cure her.

When her mother realised she was going to die, she remembered the mirror and was afraid that, after her death, her daughter would find the mirror and, just as she herself had done years before, would be filled with pride when she discovered her own beauty. She was afraid that her daughter, so young and tender, would grow foolish, shallow and vain from looking at her own image in the mirror.

She called her daughter to her side, told her where she had put the box containing the mirror, and asked her to fetch it.

When the girl returned, her mother told her to set the box down beside her, then said: 'I am going to die, but after my death, you will still be able to see me as often as you wish. I am leaving you this box, which contains my living portrait. It's called a mirror. For now, keep the box here. But after my death put it in your room. And whenever you wish to see me, you need only open the box and take out the mirror. I will appear to you in the mirror and will smile at you when you smile at me. And thus I will always be with you, and you will remember me every day. Do this in secret. It is a secret between you and me.'

The woman died shortly afterwards, and the house became very silent and empty.

The father would weep and clutch his daughter tightly to him, then retreat to his room to meditate.

True to her word, the girl went to fetch the lacquer box and took it to her room. She knelt on the mat, opened the box, removed the mirror, and looked. Just as she had been told, her mother's face appeared before her, but it was not pale and tired as it had been only recently. This was the young, beautiful mother of her childhood, with transparent skin, coral-pink lips and dark, lustrous hair. She smiled and her mother smiled back, and the two of them continued to gaze at each other for quite some time.

From then on, every night, at the hour of silence and quiet contemplation, the girl would open the box and, kneeling on the mat, would gaze at that sweet, wonderful face.

One spring evening, the girl's father, strolling

on the verandah, passed by her room. Looking in, he was surprised to see his darling little girl talking and smiling before the mirror.

'How very strange!' thought the man.

He went into the room and asked his daughter what she was doing.

'I'm talking to my mother,' she said. 'She left me her living portrait, which she called a mirror.'

She told her father how her mother had left her the box, adding: 'Every night, my mother comes to see me, but she doesn't come to me looking pale and sickly as she was at the end. She looks young and beautiful, as beautiful as she was when I was a child.'

When she finished speaking, the girl saw two tears running down her father's weary face.

For he was weeping in amazement at such a fine example of filial obedience, love and devotion.

Recommended Reading

If you have enjoyed reading *The Girl from the Sea and other stories* you should enjoy reading the other Young Dedalus titles and the *Take Six* anthology which contains stories by Sophia de Mello Breyner Andresen:

Nobody can stop Don Carlo - Oliver Scherz
Memoirs of a Basque Cow - Bernardo Atxaga
The Books that devoured my Father - Afonso Cruz
Take Six - edited by Margaret Jull Costa

If you like magic, myth, fairy tales and stories about animals you should enjoy:

The Adventures of the Ingenious Alfanhui - Rafael Sanchez Ferlosio
The Fables of Ivan Krylov - Ivan Krylov
The Cat - Pat Gray
Market Farm - Nicholas Bradbury

These books can be bought from your local bookshop or online retailer or direct from Dedalus, either online or by post. Please go to our website www.dedalusbooks.com for further details.

Nobody can stop Don Carlo - Oliver Scherz

Carlo misses his father. His parents are separated, he is with his mother in Germany while his father is back in their native Palermo. His father is always about to visit but somehow never quite gets to Germany. Carlo gets tired of waiting and decides to do something about it and sets off for Palermo but without any money to pay his fare. What happens is a series of adventures when anything that could go wrong does but Carlo despite everything gets to Palermo and lands up at his Papa's door.

Will reality live up to Carlo's dreams? This story, from Germany's leading children's author, will strike a chord with many readers as they take Carlo into their hearts.

£7.99 ISBN 978 1 912868 02 5 96p B. Format

Memoirs of a Basque Cow - Bernardo Atxaga

One dark and stormy night, Mo hears her Inner Voice urging her to begin writing her memoirs. Having ignored her Inner Voice's advice once before, with near-fatal consequences, she decides, this time, to do as she is told. Mo looks back on her life, beginning with the crucial moment when she met another cow, who introduced herself as *La Vache qui Rit,* and assured Mo that there was nothing more stupid in this world than a stupid cow. Mo spends her life trying to prove to her friend that, despite being a cow, she is not at all stupid. Besides, she has her Inner Voice and a great desire to live! Set in the aftermath of the Spanish Civil War, in which defeated Republican supporters are still being persecuted by victorious Nationalists.

Memoirs of a Basque Cow paints a funny, touching portrait of friendship and freedom and the sometimes-difficult process of finding oneself.

Translated by one of the UK's finest and most acclaimed translators: Margaret Jull Costa.

£9.99 ISBN 978 1 912868 01 8 221p B. Format

The Books that devoured my Father - Afonso Cruz

The Books that devoured my Father is a celebration of filial love, friendship and literature.

Vivaldo Bonfim was a bored book-keeper whose main escape from the tedium of his work was provided by novels. In the office, he tended to read rather than work, and, one day, became so immersed in a book that he got lost and disappeared completely. That, at least, is the version given to Vivaldo's son, Elias, by his grandmother. One day, Elias sets off, like a modern-day Telemachus, in search of the father he never knew. His journey takes him through the plots of many classic novels, replete with murders, all-consuming passions, wild beasts and other literary perils.

Translated by one of the UK's finest and most acclaimed translators: Margaret Jull Costa.

£7.99 ISBN 978 1 912868 04 9 116p B. Format

Take Six (Six Portuguese Women Writers)
edited by Margaret Jull Costa

Take Six is a celebration of six remarkable Portuguese women writers: Sophia de Mello Breyner Andresen, Agustina Bessa-Luís, Maria Judite de Carvalho, Hélia Correia, Teolinda Gersão and Lídia Jorge.

They are all past mistresses of the short story form, and their subject matter ranges from finding one's inner fox to a failed suicide attempt to a grandmother and grandson battling the wind on a beach. Stories and styles are all very different, but what the writers have in common is their ability to take everyday life and look at it afresh, so that even a trip on a ferry or an encounter with a stranger or a child's attempt to please her father become imbued with mystery and humour and sometimes tragedy. Relatively few women writers are translated into English, and this anthology is an attempt to rectify that imbalance and to introduce readers to some truly captivating tales from Portugal.

£9.99 ISBN 978 1 910213 69 8 252p B. Format

The Adventures of the Ingenious Alfanhuí – Rafael Sánchez Ferlosio

'Trees with feathers for leaves, birds with leaves for feathers, lizards that turn into gold, rivers of blood and transparent horses – these are just some of the magical occurrences in this enchanting fairytale. This book of wild ideas and true lies is a kaleidoscopic celebration of the natural world, and a poetic parable on the passage from innocence to experience.'

Lisa Allardice in *The Independent on Sunday*

'A boy's adventurous quest for knowledge is the subject of this classic 'children's fantasy for adults,' the first (1952) and most famous novel produced by an eminent Spanish author later better known as an essayist and linguist. The resourceful Alfanhuí – part Candide, part Tom Swift, and just possibly an ironic Christ figure – is an apprentice scientist and magician whose picaresque adventures in urban Madrid and rural Spain are simultaneously acts of creation (such as 'creating water out of light'), healing, and homage to the inexorable mysteriousness of the physical world. A highly unusual novel, and a thoroughly engaging one.' *Kirkus Reviews*

'In his dedication, Ferlosio describes this exquisite fantasy novel, first published in 1952 and now beautifully translated into English as a "story full of true lies". Much honored in his native Spain, Ferlosio is a fabulist comparable to Jorge Borges and Italo Calvino, as well as Joan Miro and Salvador Dali. Cervantes comes to mind. Ferlosio's prose is effortlessly evocative. A chair puts down roots and sprouts "a few green branches and some cherries", while a paint-absorbing tree becomes a "marvelous botanical harlequin". Later, Alfanhuí sets off on a tour of Castile, meeting his aged grandmother "who incubated chicks in her lap and had a vine trellis of muscatel grapes and who never died". This is a haunting adult reverie on life and beauty and as such will appeal to discriminating readers.'

Starred review in *Publishers Weekly*

£9.99 ISBN 978 1 910213 82 7 199p B. Format

The Fables of Ivan Krylov - Ivan Krylov

Ivan Krylov has been loved by Russian people for two hundred years for his Fables, works in which he gently satirizes the manifold weaknesses and failings of human beings, especially figures of authority, while at the same time praising and holding up for emulation the qualities in ordinary people of selflessness, industry, loyalty, love, friendship, perseverance…

Solid, earthy common sense and a long acquaintance with the ways of the world lie at the root of Krylov's observations. Some of the Fables are no more than humorous glimpses of life and human nature, or snapshots of the bizarre preoccupations of fantasists, eccentrics, idealists and dreamers. Others offer wry, sardonic glimpses of life, and human relationships and behaviour. Yet others offer wise advice on the conduct of life, or are 'cautionary tales': warnings about the consequences of ill-considered behaviour.

Like other great allegorical writings, the Fables can be read on different levels, and enjoyed by all, from young children to the very old.

£9.99 ISBN 978 1 910213 51 3 268p B. Format

The Cat - Pat Gray

Pat Gray's classic tale of friendship between the Cat, Mouse and Rat will appeal to lovers of books about cats and animal fables.

'Left in an empty house, the Cat - previously pampered with canned food and his owners' affection - learns to hunt again, much to the alarm of the intellectual Mouse and the proletarian, politically aware Rat. As Cat makes inroads into the garden (renting property to voles, for example, and thus discouraging their allegiance with those who would topple him), Mouse and Rat try to stave off the Cat's despotic rise. They discover the Cat's vulnerable area: he hungers not only for the deference of the various rodents he has cowed but also for the affection of humans that he once knew. Gray's satire thus at first seems to target the amorality of the ruling classes, only to turn its attention more squarely to capitalism - the hollow repast that never satisfies, the empty acquisition of material goods.' *Publishers Weekly*

'Gray's reworking of the *Animal Farm* concept brings in a post-Thatcherite twist. Having peacefully co-existed with his friends Mouse and Rat (the latter carries a briefcase and wears Italian suits), the Cat's owners suddenly leave him to fend for himself. He then has to fall back on feline instincts, placating the furry packed lunches which surround him with promises of consumer goods and burrow ownership. A stylish and witty parable.'

Scotland on Sunday

'*The Cat* is a dark and amusing political allegory about Cat, Rat, and Mouse, and how they get along after the sudden death of the Professor. After the Professor falls dead at the fridge, having stuffed himself with desserts, and lies like the statue of Ozymandias on the kitchen lino, his face lathered with whipped cream, Rat and Mouse climb over the body and invade the open fridge. Next day, Mrs. Professor has the body removed and later sells the house and moves out. Suddenly, the place is swept clean, and Rat, arising like a labor leader, tries to organize the house on new principles, without Cat having the top post. Mouse, a spineless intellectual, is Rat's assistant – until he gets fed up and disappears. While Rat organizes the garden creatures, Cat falls in with Tom, who finds every night a good night for girls. "Pussy!" he purrs with a low growl. Then Cat takes up television and learns to speak like a human to the house's new owner, Mrs. Digby. Eventually, Cat takes over again, asking, "D'ye think Rat knows about accounts?" Cat is back, in Mrs. Digby's lap, while Rat and Mouse turn grey like old pensioners. Gray's characters amuse in their parody of human beings.' *Kirkus Reviews*

£8.99 ISBN 978 1 910213 36 0 124p B. Format

Market Farm – Nicholas Bradbury

'Like *Animal Farm, Market Farm* is run by the pigs, although elections allow the other animals to decide whether the pink or blue porcine faction should be in charge. This benevolent pseudo-democracy is accepted by the populace, as "prosperity for all" is both promised and delivered. Enter the foxes who, after gaining the other animals' trust, persuade the pigs that the farm is being run inefficiently, and introduce market forces, and an increasing number of exciting financial products, into play. All this is seen through the eyes of Merlin, the Eeyore-like donkey, who distrusts the hype yet is quite the entrepreneur, and his friends Errol, the optimistic bull, and Lily, the ditsy and so easily confused chicken. *Market Farm* should be a set text for all students of politics and economics.' Scarlett McCGwire in *Tribune*

£8.99 ISBN 978 1 909232 55 6 144p B. Format

Young Dedalus 2020